Rosa

*A
Harlequin
Romance*

WELCOME

TO THE WONDERFUL WORLD

of Harlequin Romances!

Interesting, informative and entertaining,
each Harlequin Romance portrays an appealing
love story. Harlequin Romances take you
to faraway places — places with real people
facing real love situations — and
you become part of their story.

As publishers of Harlequin Romances, we're extremely
proud of our books (we've been publishing
them since 1954). We're proud also that Harlequin
Romances are North America's most-read
paperback romances.

Eight new titles are released every month and are
sold at nearly all book-selling stores across
Canada and the United States.

A free catalogue listing all available Harlequin Romances
can be yours by writing to the

HARLEQUIN READER SERVICE,
M.P.O. Box 707, Niagara Falls, N.Y. 14302.
Canadian address: Stratford, Ontario, Canada.

or use order coupon at back of book.

We sincerely hope you enjoy reading
this Harlequin Romance.

Yours truly,

THE PUBLISHERS
    Harlequin Romances

FOLLOW
A STRANGER

by

CHARLOTTE LAMB

HARLEQUIN BOOKS TORONTO
WINNIPEG

Original hard cover edition published in 1973
by Mills & Boon Limited.

© Charlotte Lamb 1973

SBN 373-01722-7

Harlequin edition published October 1973

Printed in Canada

1722

CHAPTER ONE

THERE had been a frost overnight, leaving the grass white and sparkling in the early morning sunshine. When Kate looked out of her window, at seven, pearly mist obscured her view, and she dressed quickly, shivering, hoping that it was not going to be another grey day. But at nine, when she left the house, the wind had blown the mist away, and the sky was a bright, clear blue.

The change lifted her spirits. She walked along slowly, her dreamy eyes fixed on the elm tree tops which showed above Cheddall's walls, swaying slowly against the heavenly blue of the sky. The black branches were thickened by rooks' nests and as she watched some of the ungainly black birds rose up, cawing.

The sound reminded her of summer. She shivered, clutching her coat closer. Despite the sunshine it was still a chilly January morning.

Still dreaming, she stepped into the road, and was dragged down to earth by the blare of a car horn. She leapt back to the pavement and looked round, heart pounding.

A sleek black car had pulled up, brakes screeching dramatically. The driver got out and walked round to her. "What the devil do you think you're doing, walking under my wheels like that?"

Kate had the impression of looking up a long way

to his dark, angry face. "I'm sorry," she stammered. "It was my fault, I know. But," her nerves shaken by his harsh tones, "there's no need to shout at me like that."

"You must expect people to lose their temper if you try to commit suicide under their cars," he retorted. "Are you hurt?"

"No, thank you," she said, in the same angry tone he had used for the question.

"You needn't sound so aggrieved," he snapped, staring at her, "I'm the one with a grievance, I think."

"I've said I'm sorry. What more do you want?"

"You sound sorry," he said sarcastically.

Her hair bristled on the back of her neck. "I was very sorry at first, but your attitude would put anyone's back up."

"Women!" he grunted. "How very logical! Well, if you're not hurt, good morning."

She watched him stride back to his car and felt like childishly stamping her foot. Male superiority triumphs again, she thought, as he drove past without a second glance. Men like that would make the mildest female join Women's Lib!

She glanced at her watch and was horrified to see the time. She would be late if she did not hurry and her first lesson was at nine-fifteen. She crossed the road, looking both ways, and ran the rest of the way to the school.

The summons to Miss Carter's study came while Kate was listening to a first-former attempting to play the piano. Both pupil and teacher sighed with relief at the interruption. Kate grinned as she followed the reluctant pianist out of the music room. If only parents knew what resentments they bred in their children when they forced them to take up music against their inclination!

It was true, of course, that sometimes they developed an interest at a later stage and were then grateful for their early grounding. But, somehow, she did not think that this would apply to the girl scuttling eagerly in front of her. Lucy Salmon had fingers like sausages and was almost totally tone-deaf. Her musical father was doomed to disappointment.

She paused at a pale primrose door and knocked softly.

"Come in," Miss Carter commanded, and when Kate entered, smiled at her across the pleasant, sunny room.

"Ah, my dear. I'm sorry to disturb you during a lesson, but I'm leaving shortly to lunch with the Mayor, and I wanted to discuss something with you. Sit down."

The Headmistress of Cheddall Public School for Girls was as pleasant as her room. Sensible, sandy-haired and blue-eyed, she had an enviable calm which Kate had never seen ruffled. Her appointment last year, at the early age of forty, had surprised no one. She had been acting as deputy for the previous five years with great success and was popular with parents and girls alike.

Some of the staff had disapproved of the changes she had made, others had heartily supported her. But there were few people who disliked her.

Kate sat back, wondering what she had done wrong. A summons to the Head was usually a sign of the wrath to come, but she could not remember having fallen from grace lately, so she smiled and waited patiently.

She was unaware, being a very modest girl, that when she smiled two dimples appeared in her cheeks, or that her eyes had a warmth in their depths which usually produced a responsive smile from the people she was with, but she was relieved to see Miss Carter smile back.

Leaning forward with her square hands laid flat on her desk, the Headmistress said, "We expect a new pupil tomorrow, Kate." She paused, as if searching for the right words. "Rather a special case." Then paused again, as if anticipating questions.

Kate nodded. If a girl was alolwed to join the school in the middle of a term it must, indeed, be a special case, but since the Head clearly wanted some reply, she said politely, "Yes, Miss Carter?"

The Head laughed. "I'll be frank—I feel rather doubtful about accepting this girl." She shook her head and stared at the window in silence for a moment. "She's hardly the sort of girl we normally have here." She paused again and began to sketch a queer little doodle, then, without looking up, added, "Her brother is Marc Lillitos."

Kate blinked. Who was he? Clearly she was expected to know the name, but although she searched her memory, she could never remember having heard it before.

Miss Carter looked up, her eyes curious. "You do not know the name?"

"No," Kate admitted.

"He's a shipping magnate, a very wealthy man.

He came to me today and asked me to accept his sister Pallas. . . ."

"Pallas!" Kate interrupted, without thinking.

Miss Carter smiled. "Pallas Athene, the Greek goddess of wisdom, but I'm afraid the name does not fit this girl. She has been expelled from three really excellent schools already."

"Goodness!" exclaimed Kate, in amazement.

"Quite. As you know, we don't take problem children here at Cheddall, so I hesitated. But her brother assures me that, despite the evidence, she is a talented and clever girl, and he convinced me that she deserves a final chance. After a long discussion, I agreed, but on my own conditions." She paused again, frowning. "That's where you come in, Kate."

Kate nodded, "Yes?"

"I gathered that she is in rebellion against the discipline of school. She wants to go to a college of music, where she feels she'll have more freedom."

"She's musical?" Kate said, seeing now how this affected herself.

"Very, it appears. She both plays the violin and sings. But her family want her to have a sound education before she specialises. I sensed vague disapproval of a musical career, but nothing was said on that subject."

"If they're rich, I wouldn't have thought it would matter," said Kate.

"They probably fear she will make the wrong friends. I suspect they give her very little freedom at home. A strict background, strict schools—you can see the pattern."

9

Kate grimaced. "Only too clearly. What do you want me to do, Miss Carter?"

The Head smiled. "Make friends with her."

"Of course," Kate agreed. "But as I live out of school that may not be easy."

"On the contrary, it's an advantage. It gives you a less claustrophobic attitude to the school. It might be an idea to take her to your home, let her have a taste of ordinary home life. Boarding schools tend to narrow one's horizons. I realise it's asking a great deal, Kate. You would prefer to get away from school when you're off duty. But I feel sorry for the girl."

"So do I," said Kate.

"Well, don't let her suspect that, will you? I would prefer the relationship to develop quite naturally. Pity would only make matters worse. The poor little rich girl theme is poisonous."

Kate laughed. "I understand. I think I can handle it."

"Good." Miss Carter smiled at her. "Thank you, Kate."

Kate Caulfield was twenty-four, slightly built, with long straight blonde hair, unusually vivid blue eyes, and the strong flexible fingers of a pianist.

She had trained in London, and had had dreams of being a concert pianist, but since she was a practical girl beneath her dreamy exterior, she soon realised that she did not have the necessary ability.

When she left college she accepted the post of music teacher at Cheddall Public School, since it was only a few minutes' walk from her home.

Since Miss Carter became Headmistress the school

had been reorganised on more modern lines. There was less severity, more freedom, and the girls seemed to thrive upon the new régime. Kate was very happy there, especially since it left her with plenty of free time in which to be with her fiancé, Peter Hardy.

Peter ran the local museum and, in his own spare time, was an ardent archaeologist. Kate had known him all her life.

Her father had died five years earlier, leaving his wife with four children to bring up. Kate's salary was the only family income for the present, since her younger brother, Sam, was studying art at the local art school, and her twin brothers, Harry and John, were only eleven.

That evening she told her mother about Pallas Lillitos while they washed up after supper.

Sam listened idly, sitting astride a chair, eating a bag of peanuts.

"She sounds a real frost," he remarked, "spoilt and conceited."

"Didn't you have enough supper?" Kate countered. "You eat as if you never expected to see another meal!"

He grinned, wrinkling his freckled nose at her. Sam had red hair, big ears and an inexhaustible passion for food. Only his blue eyes were any reminder of the fact that they were brother and sister.

"You're just jealous because I don't have to diet to keep my figure."

She threw the tea-towel at him. "How true, you abominable boy!"

Mrs. Caulfield smiled, her gaze resting on Kate's trim waist. "You don't need to diet either, Kate."

Kate put her hands on either side of her waist, sighing. "I do if I want to wear my new dress for the spring dance at the Tennis Club. I need to lose an inch off my waist, or the dress will burst at the seams."

"You should have bought a larger size," said her mother.

"They only had it in one size and it was too gorgeous to resist."

"It cost a bomb, too," Sam said. "Which reminds me—lend me a quid, Kate. I want to take Karen to the pictures."

Kate groaned, but produced the money. "I thought girls went dutch these days."

"Not Karen," he said proudly. "Half the male population of Greyford is trying to date her. I wouldn't dare suggest we go dutch."

When he had vanished to change into even sloppier jeans, his mother laughed. "Karen isn't a girl—she's a prize. Sam is delighted to be dating her."

"I can't think why," said Kate. "She's the most boring girl I ever met."

"But she looks like a beauty queen," said Mrs. Caulfield with amusement, "and all the other boys are crazy about her."

The doorbell rang and Kate jumped up. "That will be Peter—I'll go."

She opened the door and a tall, bearded young man wandered in, smiling vaguely at her. "Hi!"

She sighed and reached up to kiss him. "Hello, darling. Had an interesting day?"

He looked almost lively. "Yes—guess what was brought in? Another urn fragment from the Roman fort at Lower Greyford. And it fits perfectly! The urn is really taking shape now. Another few pieces and I'll have a complete second-century urn."

"How fascinating, darling. Like a jigsaw puzzle," she said, pushing him into the sitting-room.

Peter Hardy was a few years older than Kate, but looked less, because his features were less mature. Sam had once said that Peter looked like a Viking, talked like a professor and hardly knew one girl from another. Blond, grey-eyed and pleasant, he was too passionately involved with his work to be aware of anything else.

Kate, who had fallen in love with him years ago and had only managed to make him notice her by being continually underfoot, often wondered if he remembered that they were engaged to be married. Certainly he never suggested a wedding date. But she curled up beside him on the sofa and let him talk of Roman urns while her mind wandered to more romantic ideas.

A few days later Miss Carter came into the music room and introduced her to Pallas Lillitos.

Kate was taken aback to find her new pupil to be far more adult than she had expected. She was wearing a plain black skirt and white blouse, the usual sixth form version of the school uniform. But she managed to invest it with a Parisian chic which, with her sleek black hair and matt complexion, made her look nearer twenty than sixteen.

Miss Carter left them alone together after a moment or two, and Kate looked thoughtfully at the new girl.

13

"Perhaps you'd better show me what you can do," she suggested. "Shall we start with the violin?"

Pallas shrugged indifferently. Taking out her violin, she played a dazzling piece of Paganini, her face remote and austere beneath her black cap of hair.

Kate smiled at her when she had finished. She knew very well that Pallas had chosen that particular piece in order to startle her by her technical brilliance, and, she had to admit, it was very clever. But there had been something lacking. She could not quite put her finger on what that was, but she said nothing, except to ask Pallas to sing for her.

The girl looked a little cross. Sullenly she chose a song, Kate played the introduction on the piano, and Pallas sang.

Kate's fingers almost halted in amazement as the clear, sweet notes spilled out. She looked round and saw a dreamy expression stealing into the girl's face.

Afterwards, she closed the piano lid with a gesture of finality. "You don't need me to tell you that you have a very lovely voice," she said, smiling at Pallas. "I shall arrange for our specialist violin teacher to come in and teach you. Your voice is really almost beyond me. You need serious training."

"When I am eighteen Marc will let me go to a college of music," said the girl. "But he has no intention of letting me take up a professional career. So what does it matter?"

Kate leaned back and stared at her. "Why won't he let you become a musician?"

"He wants me to marry," said Pallas, "as I'm sure you know!" And her eyes bit contemptuously at Kate.

"How should I know? I've never met him. Why shouldn't you marry and still have a career?"

Pallas shrugged, without answering.

Kate waited, then changed the subject. "I'm sure Miss Carter could arrange to have someone really good to come in and teach you singing. Madame Liovitch lives twenty miles away—she might accept you as a pupil."

Pallas looked at Kate for a while, frowning. "No," she said, at last, "I want you to teach me."

"Me?" Kate was absurdly touched. "My dear girl, I'm not fit to black Madame Liovitch's shoes. I really think you could teach me rather than the other way around."

Pallas smiled, with sudden and surprising charm. "I'll take the risk."

"Why?" Kate asked curiously.

Pallas flushed. "I . . . I like you. You seem honest."

The friendship between them grew quickly. Kate had no real friends on the staff, since she lived out, and Pallas found the other girls far too schoolgirlish for her. She asked Kate about her family, and was very amused by the descriptions of Sam, Harry and John.

"Sam's a nut case," Kate explained.

"What's that?" asked Pallas, and when it was translated, went off into peals of laughter.

Kate invited her to visit them and was touched by the eagerness of the girl's acceptance. It occurred to her to wonder what the autocratic Marc Lillitos would think if he knew that Miss Carter was encouraging his sheltered little sister to visit an ordinary family.

He sounded like a tyrannical paterfamilias, a type which she had thought extinct years ago.

When Pallas appeared at the Caulfield home she was wearing a chic grey dress, pretty grey shoes which looked hand-made and very expensive, and a very smart hat on her black hair.

Sam, lounging on the carpet with his head on a cushion, gazed at her as though at a very rare and peculiar animal. Kate introduced her to the assembled family, and made her sit down on the sofa. There was a difficult silence.

Then the twins, rarely at a loss for long, politely offered her one of their awful jokes, and were pleased, if surprised, when she laughed. Thus encouraged, they told a succession of them. Pallas, conscious of Sam's unrelenting stare, laughed at each with as much enjoyment.

Mrs Caulfield disappeared into the kitchen, and the twins, drawn by the sound of cakes coming out of the oven, drifted after her.

"Have you any younger brothers?" Sam asked pointedly.

Pallas looked round, as though amazed to find him present, "No, but I have an older brother," she said. "I did have two, but one died three years ago."

"I'm sorry," said Kate.

Pallas said honestly, "I did not know him very well. He lived in America. His wife still does."

Mrs. Caulfield called Kate who, excusing herself, left the two young people alone.

Pallas sat up very straight, her hands in her lap, like a little girl at a grown-up tea-party. Sam lay back, staring at the ceiling. She furtively inspected

16

him from his red sweater to his purple, fringed velvet trousers, then back, with widened eyes, to the brown-red curls which fell to his shoulders in wild abandon.

He turned his head lazily and stared back until her eyes fell and she flushed.

"What's with the gear?" he asked obscurely.

"I'm sorry?" She jumped and looked bewildered.

"The clothes," he translated. "Why are you wearing that drag?"

In a flash of temper she retorted, "I look no stranger than you do. I couldn't make up my mind whether you were a girl or a boy."

He laughed and leapt up, in one supple movement. Bending over her, he kissed her mouth before she was aware of his intention.

She gasped, backing away.

"Give you three guesses," he offered wickedly.

Bright pink, she said crossly, "Don't ever do that again!"

"Go on," teased Sam, "you know you loved it! I bet that was the first time you were ever kissed!"

She bit her lip in fury. Brought up in an atmosphere of luxurious reverence, she was not accustomed to boys like Sam. She was as sheltered as a novice from a convent school. Sam baffled, alarmed, fascinated her.

Over the following weeks she became a fixture in the Caulfield home. She and Kate shopped together and Pallas bought a number of new clothes, with an eye to surprising Sam. Jeans, bright cotton sweaters, mini skirts and flared trousers were added to her wardrobe week by week. The neat, Paris-made suits and dresses were pushed aside. She flowered out into vivid colours, wild designs, and heavy, esoteric jewellery.

Sam whistled admiringly when she arrived one day in an emerald green dress made of silky clinging material, which ended way above her knees, revealing long brown legs. She looked much younger, much prettier, more alive.

"You're quite a little dolly," he complimented her, and Kate, seeing her blush scarlet, suddenly wondered if she was wise in allowing their friendship to develop. Her family would undoubtedly disapprove. Yet she did not have the heart to cut Pallas out of the family. The girl was so clearly happy. The sullen look which she had always worn at first was never seen now. Her school work had improved enormously since Sam made a few pointed remarks about the dignity of labour. Sam worked very hard himself and had no time for those who shirked.

Pallas had never enjoyed the casual, cheerful atmosphere of an ordinary home before, and Kate suspected that if it was taken away from her now, the girl would be twice as unhappy.

Her interest in Sam was unfortunate, but Kate knew her brother too well to fear any romantic entanglement. He was level-headed, kind, ambitious. The glamour girls of his world amused him, but he would not let himself get involved seriously while he was still at art school, especially since he knew that his mother and brothers would need his economic support later.

She was convinced that she was right some weeks later when she watched Sam and Pallas dancing to a record. Pallas was tense, nervous, clumsy as she tried to follow him.

"You're too uptight," he complained. "You dance as if you had a poker stuck up your back."

Pallas went bright red. "You beast!" she shouted, pushing at his chest.

Sam laughed and grabbed her by the shoulders.

"Stop the fireworks! Try it again, and put some give into it this time!"

Pallas did better this time, and Sam grinned at her, "You're getting the message! That was better!"

She beamed at him, her black hair loose and swinging. She was a totally different girl from the one who had first visited them. Today she wore bright yellow jeans, an orange sweater with Mickey Mouse appliquéd on the front, and an Egyptian enamelled pendant which gave her an Oriental look.

They danced again, not touching each other, gyrating like strange birds performing a ritual mating ceremony.

Kate watched, grinning. The veneer of maturity had been stripped away from Pallas, leaving her a normal teenager.

When the music ended this time, Sam hugged Pallas, in a friendly way. "Great, kid! You can really swing!"

And she, flushed and excited, threw her arms around him. "Oh, Sam, do you think so?"

Kate heard the door open and glanced round, casually, expecting to see her mother. But a tall man in the doorway, his gaze fixed icily on the two in the middle of the room, who were too absorbed in each other to have noticed him.

Kate recognised him. It was the man under whose car she had almost committed suicide.

Then Pallas glanced over Sam's shoulder, froze, and dropped her arms as if they had suddenly developed paralysis.

Sam turned and stared curiously at the intruder, who stared back, his thick black brows meeting over his nose.

"Well, Pallas?" he asked coolly. "Aren't you going to introduce me to your . . . friends?" The hesitation was deliberate, and insulting.

A flash of intuition told Kate who this man was before Pallas spoke, and she got up nervously.

He looked round, grey eyes hard, and studied her. Forcing herself to look calm, she looked back, and saw a man of thirty or so, very self-assured, his features arrogantly good-looking, his clothes discreetly well cut. He was as dark as Pallas, his black hair thick and straight, his skin very tanned.

Pallas came forward awkwardly, as white now as she had been red, and falteringly introduced Kate.

Kate held out her hand, making herself smile, but Marc Lillitos took it with a firm grip, unsmilingly.

Then he looked at Sam. Pallas mumbled Sam's name. Kate was very proud of her brother as he came forward, suddenly dignified, and shook hands. He did not allow the older man to stare him out of countenance, but met his eyes directly and frankly.

There was a brief silence, then Marc Lillitos said coldly, "Wait for me in the car, Pallas. I want to have a word with Miss Caulfield."

She stumbled out of the room with the old sullen

uncertainty back in force. Kate felt a sting of anger against this man.

Sam took Kate's elbow. "Shall I stay, Sis?"

She was grateful for his offer of support, but shook her head. "No, thank you."

Sam met her eyes, grimaced and left the room.

Marc Lillitos looked at her, very slowly and carefully, as though inspecting a loathsome slug found in his lettuce.

"I was surprised when I was informed that my sister was at your house," he began coolly. "I was horrified when I came in here and saw her, looking like some hippie, apparently kissing your brother. Have you any explanation of why you have encouraged her to behave in this disgusting way, or must I draw my own conclusions?"

Kate went scarlet. "Is it disgusting to dress like other teenagers, to learn to dance, to enjoy herself?" She found it hard to find the words to say what she wanted to say, under the steely and contemptuous gaze of this man.

"You would like me to believe, I suppose, that her money had nothing to do with it?" he asked coldly.

"Of course it didn't! I was sorry for her!"

His lips twitched mirthlessly. "Sorry for her? Envied her, you mean. Let me make some facts clear. Pallas is my ward. Her money is tied up in a trust. If she married without my consent she gets not a penny of that money. Do you understand?"

A tidal wave of rage swept over her as she listened. She drew a deep breath and launched into a flood of angry words.

"If you are implying that my brother might try

21

to marry her for her money then let me tell you a few facts about him—he's proud, hard-working and kind-hearted, and far too busy trying to date much sexier girls to be aware of Pallas as anything other than a kid sister. Like me, he was sorry for her, as he would be for any girl who wears square, old-fashioned clothes, has no fun and feels it would be better to be dead. You've stifled Pallas all her life. You buy her safe, dull, expensive clothes which she hates and which make her look ridiculous to her own generation. You shut her away in safe, dull, expensive schools rather than let her find out what life is really like. I suppose you'll take her away from Cheddall now, and put her in another tidy little box where she'll die from lack of air."

Her blue eyes shot flames at him. "Well, Mr. Lillitos, sir, your money doesn't interest us." She curtsied exaggeratedly. "Nothing about you interests us, Mr. Lillitos, sir. But next time you look at Pallas remember she's an ordinary teenager of sixteen, not a nun, and think what you're doing to her!" She walked to the door and held it open, glaring at Sam, who shot her a grin before vanishing down the hall. "Goodbye, Mr. Lillitos. It may sound trite, but your money is just a millstone round your sister's neck. So give her a chance to find out what sort of human being she really is, and stop trying to force her into an iron mould marked Lillitos."

He stared in total silence, as she spat out the last words, then walked out of the room.

CHAPTER TWO

WHEN he had gone she sat down on a chair, feeling her legs giving way beneath her, and tried to stop herself trembling. Now that her blind rage had faded, she was ashamed of herself. He would certainly take Pallas away from Cheddall after her outburst, and all the good they had tried to do would be undone.

The thought of Pallas made her mouth go down at the corners. Poor girl. No wonder she had lacked self-confidence, always being reminded by Big Brother that men were only interested in her money, never in herself. It would sap anyone's self-respect.

Sam came in, grinning, and hugged her. "You were fantastic! I was proud of you! He came out of here like a jet-propelled rocket. I bet no one ever told him a home truth before in his luxury-padded life!"

"Oh, Sam," she wailed, "but what have I done to Pallas? If only I hadn't lost my temper!"

Sam's face fell. "I'd forgotten that angle. You reckon he'll take her away from the school?"

"I'd gamble my year's salary on it!"

She did not sleep very well that night. She lay, taut and anxious, mentally rehearsing an apology to Marc Lillitos, but each time choking as she opened her mouth and saw, in her mind's eye, that arrogant dark face. After all, he had insulted Sam! And she was not really sorry for anything she had said. It had all been true. She just regretted having said it so force-fully.

She thumped her pillow irritably. What a pity he had come at that particular moment. She was certain neither Pallas nor Sam were emotionally involved with each other. It was just friendship. But to a man like Marc Lillitos a friendly hug looked like moral depravity.

She arrived at Cheddall very early next day, anticipating a summons to Miss Carter's study. The Head would quite rightly feel she had behaved very stupidly in her response to the situation. She could have been more tactful. The trouble was, thought Kate wryly, that although she had blonde hair, she had inherited her redheaded father's blazing temper. As a child she had often had lectures from him on the subject, no less stern because he fully understood her problem.

"I have a temper, too, Kate," he used to say, "but one must learn to control *it*, rather than let *it* control you."

It was odd that Sam, who had his father's hair, had been by-passed by the family temper. He was a very good-natured boy.

She waited all morning in suspense, but no summons came. Her discreet enquiries in the staff-room told her that Pallas was still at the school, and no one seemed aware of any trouble concerning her.

Had Miss Carter persuaded her brother to leave her at school? Or had he changed his mind last night, after all? Puzzled, anxious and uneasy, Kate waited all day, but when she left that afternoon she had still heard nothing.

As she turned out of the drive she heard a voice calling her name, and looked round in surprise.

The sleek black car was drawn up at the kerb and Marc Lillitos was leaning out of the window.

"I want a word with you," he said brusquely. "Get in."

Despite all her good intentions, she stiffened resentfully. Who did he think he was? His tone was as arrogant as ever. "I'm sorry," she said coldly, "I'm in a hurry."

His grey eyes were sardonic. "Then it will be quicker to go by car," he pointed out, opening the passenger door for her.

"I prefer to walk," she said, turning away.

The door slammed and suddenly he was beside her, taking her elbow in fingers which gripped painfully. "Don't be ridiculous! I want to talk to you."

"Are you kidnapping me?" she asked, her eyes flashing. "Let go of my arm—you're hurting me! How dare you? Just because you're a millionaire it doesn't give you the right to order me around."

He stared down at her, eyes amused. "What a little spitfire you are, aren't you?" he murmured. "Come, must I go down on my knees to you before you will consent to get into the car? Be reasonable, Miss Caulfield. Let me drive you home so that we can talk quietly without causing a scene."

She looked around and saw several passers-by halting, watching them curiously. Very pink, feeling very silly, she gave up the unequal struggle and allowed him to help her into the car. He climbed in and silently started the engine. Purring smoothly, the car moved away up the road.

"I wanted to apologise to you," he said quietly, staring at the road ahead.

She looked sideways at him. The long, arrogant profile was turned towards her, the droop of the eyelids hiding the expression of the hard eyes.

Since she did not reply, he shot her another of his amused looks, one eyebrow quirked. "You want your pound of flesh before you will relent, I see. Well, that is your privilege. Miss Caulfield. I unreservedly apologise. I was quite wrong in my accusations. I am very sorry for any hurt or offence I caused you or your brother."

She was too dumbfounded to speak yet, and he turned his head again, smiling at her. At the charm of that smile she felt a peculiar leap of the heart.

"Why have you changed your mind?" she asked huskily.

"I had a long talk with Miss Carter, who explained to me how much she had to do with my sister's visits to your home, and, by the way, reinforced your comments about Pallas, although more politely, I must add."

She flushed. "I . . . I'm sorry I was so rude. I lost my temper."

"So I observed," he said blandly. "But I am grateful to you for your kindness to my sister. You were very perceptive. I should have realised what was wrong myself. The trouble is, my mother has been in delicate health for a long time, and I have been too busy to take much notice of Pallas. But I had a long talk with her last night, after I had seen Miss Carter, and I hope I shall do better in the future."

"You mean to leave her at Cheddall, then?" she asked.

"Yes, I do. I cannot pretend to approve of the peculiar clothes she now wears, or her new hairstyle. She looks just like any untidy, long-haired student we get in Greece. But I did appreciate what you said about letting her become a normal adolescent, and I am prepared to put up with all this for a while." His smile was derisive. "I presume it will not last too long? I cannot guarantee a long-term indulgence."

She smiled back. "Oh, I think you can be sure that she'll grow out of it, eventually."

His eyes mocked her. "That last word was intended to frighten me, I think?"

Kate laughed. "Perhaps a little."

"You think I need to be frightened?"

"Don't we all need it, at some time or another? Pallas, at the moment, needs to be part of the scene."

He raised an enquiring eyebrow. "Translate that, please. I am not au fait with current slang."

"She needs to feel like every other person of her age—to be accepted, to merge with her background. At school, of course, she will wear school uniform, and she accepts that as normal. Out of school she wants to dress like the other kids—and that's normal, too. It's all a question of convention, although you may not think so at first sight. Long hair, jeans and bright colours *are* the teenage uniform."

"So that what I took for a gesture of rebellion is, in fact, sheep-like following of fashion?"

"Precisely," Kate said, smiling. She looked round and realised that they had been parked outside her home for some time. "I must go, now. Goodbye, Mr. Lillitos."

"Wait!" He reached across and held on to the door handle, his face close to hers. She could see faint specks of yellow around the black centres of his eyes. "I have something else I wish to discuss with you, Miss Caulfield—another matter concerning Pallas. Will you dine with me tonight?"

"I'm sorry," she said politely, "I have another engagement."

He released the door and she opened it and got out.

He leant forward, smiling with that surprising charm. "I am sure you can break your appointment just this once. I leave for Greece tomorrow and I will not have another chance to talk to you."

"Well, I . . ." she began, intending to refuse firmly.

"Good," he broke in, before she had finished. "I'll pick you up at seven-thirty."

The door slammed shut and before she could speak again, the car had drawn silently away.

Kate stared after it, clenching her fists like a child. "Well!" she exploded. "He's the most insufferable, high-handed man I ever met!"

She had had a date with Peter that night. They had intended to see a local amateur production of *Carmen*. When she rang him to explain he was irritatingly complacent.

"That's all right. I was not that keen myself. I want to finish reading Howard Carter's book on the discovery of Tutankhamen's tomb, anyway. Make sure this chap buys you a decent meal. Oh, by the way,

I think I've persuaded Colonel Feather to leave his collection of flints to the museum. Isn't that wonderful?"

She agreed flatly that it was, and rang off. Her mother looked up as she drifted into the kitchen.

"You look upset, dear. Did Peter object to you dining with Mr. Lillitos?"

"Far from it," Kate sighed. "He seemed quite pleased to have a free night to read archaeology."

Mrs. Caulfield smiled, but watched her with concern. She often wondered if Peter were the right man for Kate. They were more like brother and sister than lovers. Peter was nice enough, but rather too wrapped up in his work, and Kate was an impulsive, warm-hearted girl. It would be a tragedy if she married a man who could never respond to her. Sometimes Mrs. Caulfield had a nightmare in which Kate was buried alive, under dusty tomes, and Peter worked on, deaf to her cries for help. She shook herself mentally, and began to whip up a cream sponge. The twins would be back from school soon, ravenous and noisy.

"What are you going to wear?" she asked Kate, beating the mixture lightly.

"Goodness knows. I haven't got a dress which is even remotely suitable for dinner with a millionaire."

"Your pink one is pretty," her mother suggested.

Kate laughed at her. "My pink one, Mother, is the only formal dress I possess, as you perfectly well know!" She shrugged her shoulders. "But so what? I'm not trying to compete with the glamour girls he usually takes around, am I? It doesn't matter what he thinks of my dress."

Sam, putting his head around the door, grinned,

"There was a false ring to that remark. What are you talking about?"

Kate put out her tongue, but told him.

Sam whistled. "You must have penetrated that thick hide of his, after all! It's your big blue eyes and Goldilocks hair, Sis."

Kate was angry to feel herself blushing. "Don't be silly," she told him severely, and went upstairs to have a bath.

She took her time over her preparations and it was almost seven when she looked at herself in the mirror for the last time. Her dress was very simple, a high-waisted pink crêpe, with a scooped neckline and long, wide sleeves which floated as she moved her arms. With her blonde hair in a smooth chignon, a matching pink lipstick and her favourite false eye-lashes, she decided she looked passable.

If only she did not look so maddeningly young! She suddenly longed for a glittering sophistication. She would have liked to sweep downstairs and see his eyes open in stunned admiration.

Then she made a face at herself. What silly nonsense! They were ships, passing in the night. What did it matter what he thought of her?

She touched behind her ears with some scent, tucked back a wandering hair, and then heard his voice below. He was early! Kate felt her heart flip over peculiarly, as it had once before that day, and ordered herself to be calm and collected.

As she approached the sitting-room she heard him refuse the drink her mother was offering. She opened the door quietly. He turned to look at her, his expression inscrutable.

"Ah, there you are," he said calmly. "I am afraid I am rather early."

"It doesn't matter," she stammered, conscious of his gaze.

He took her arm and smiled at her mother. "Good night, Mrs. Caulfield."

As they drove away he said, "I thought we would dine at the Black Swan. Do you know it?"

She did, but had never been there, since it was the most expensive hotel for miles around. They drove for a quarter of an hour before reaching the high gates. The hotel was set back in its own grounds, the drive bordered by masses of rhododendron bushes which, in summer, were a blaze of colour. Now they were dimly visible, in the car headlights.

They pulled up in front of the hotel. He came round and helped her out of the car and they walked round to the brilliantly lit porch.

They were escorted to their table by an obsequious head waiter who used her host's name ostentatiously. Kate guessed that even the Black Swan was not accustomed to the patronage of such wealthy customers. Not many people in Greyford came into the supertax bracket and there were no local millionaires.

She found the punctilious attentions embarrassing. Flushed and irritable, she avoided Marc Lillitos's eyes. Was this how he was always treated? With hovering waiters; flattering, bowing and scraping; continual observation by the other guests, curious whispers at each move he made? It must be abominable.

But if it was, perhaps it went some way to explaining his air of arrogant self-assurance. How often had someone said no to him? How many times had he

31

heard angry voices? Been told the truth? In his way, he was as warped as Pallas had been, twisted out of shape by the pressures his money created around him.

She was so embarrassed that she barely tasted the meal, but it was beautifully prepared and presented. She shook her head when her host asked her to choose, and left it all to him. He ran a quick eye over the menu and chose shrimp cocktail; duck, green peas, orange sauce and game chips followed for her by a creme caramel and for himself with cheese.

She ate in almost total silence, answering only when he asked her a question, painfully aware of the stares of the other diners, and wishing herself anywhere but there.

The dining-room emptied as they reached the coffee stage and he leaned over to offer a cigarette, which she refused. He asked if she would mind if he smoked. She said that she did not, and watched him light his cigarette and push the lighter back into his pocket.

He had long, slender, shapely hands, beautifully cared for, and she stared at them with almost hypnotised awareness.

"Now," he said quietly, "shall we discuss my sister?"

Kate stared and glanced up from her contemplation of his hands, her eyes wide. "Oh, yes . . . of course."

His look held hers for a second, one dark brow raised quizzically. Then he smiled slightly.

"Part of the problem is that I have no experience of young girls. Had she been a boy I might have understood her better. My mother, as I said, is bedridden for much of the time. My sister-in-law lives in America and only visits us occasionally." He spread his hands in an expressive gesture. "So Pallas is very lonely when she is at home."

"Surely you have some young friends?" she asked, surprised.

He shook his head. "I am a very busy man. My friends are all business acquaintances."

"Doesn't Pallas have *any* friends of her own?" She was not aware of the shocked disbelief of her own voice, but he looked hard at her.

"You find that strange? Yes, it is, I suppose. When she was small she used to play with the island children, but most of the girls in her age group are married now, or will be soon. Our girls mature early."

"No wonder Pallas feels cut off," Kate said slowly. "She's sent away to school while the girls she grew up with are regarded as adult women! When she first came to Cheddall she looked so sad—a young girl dressed like a middle-aged woman, very quiet and aloof. She was marooned on an island at a time when she should have been having fun with people of her own age."

"She had her music," he protested.

"Which you don't take seriously!"

He met her eyes. "She told you that?" And when Kate nodded, he said, "She was wrong, but that can wait. First, I want to know if you really like my sister, or if you are only sorry for her."

"I like her," Kate said. "I'm sorry for her, too, but there's something appealing about her. She's so ... eager. She wants to be happy. It's touching."

"Good, I am glad you like her. I want you and Sam to visit her during the Easter holiday."

She was shocked into an exclamation. "What?" Then, flushing, "I'm sorry, I was rather surprised. . . ."

He smiled, a little teasingly, which surprised her again. She had not thought he could look so human, the dark face relaxed and friendly. "You do respond impulsively, don't you? But will you come? Our home is on Kianthos, a small Greek island. I have a private plane which will fly you there and back. Our villa is very secluded, but we have an excellent private beach, tennis courts, swimming pool—all the things young people like for a holiday."

She stared at him, feeling as unreal as a dream. "It's very kind of you . . ." she began, but again he cut her off.

"It will be a kindness in you to accept."

She shook her head. "I'm sorry, but it's impossible. I've already planned my Easter holiday."

He stubbed out his cigarette. "I would, of course, be happy to compensate you for any expense you might incur. . . ."

"Please!" she broke in angrily. "You don't understand. I'm going on a dig in Sussex, with my fiancé. I couldn't break off the arrangements now."

He leaned back, his hands lying very still on the table, palms down. "Your fiancé?" he repeated, his eyes narrowed.

Kate held up her ring finger so that he could see the Victorian opals gleaming. She and Peter had chosen the ring together. He had liked the massive gold hoop, set with milky stones, and, although Kate had preferred a small sapphire ring, she had been happy to wear the one Peter liked.

Marc Lillitos stared at the ring, face impassive. "Did you say you were going on a dig?" he repeated.

"Yes, Peter is an archaeologist. We always spend our holidays at archaeological sites."

He raised a sardonic brow. "How un-usual!" The smoothly derisive tone infuriated her once more.

"We like it!" she shot back angrily.

His smile doubted her, but he only said, "If your fiancé cares to come, too, he will be very welcome."

She shook her head. "That's very kind of you, but I'm afraid Peter wouldn't be interested."

"I'm sorry," he said. "Pallas would have been so happy to have you there, but I am sure she will understand that you prefer to be with your real friends."

"That isn't fair," she said hotly. "I like her very much, but Peter is my fiancé, after all. . . ."

"Don't worry," he said blandly, "I'll explain it to her."

"I bet you will!" she seethed, "and hurt her feelings badly in the process." She stood up. "Will you take me home now? I think we've said enough."

He did not argue. They drove home in a frozen silence. When he stopped the car she fumbled with the door and he leaned over and put his hand over hers. "I'll do it," he murmured, looking down at her with the teasing smile which had surprised her earlier.

Kate angrily realised that her heart had once again performed that peculiar, inexplicable flip. Climbing out with dignity, she said good night and then shot away as though the devil were after her.

Sam was waiting up for her, a flask of cocoa on the

kitchen table at his elbow, his sketch pad open under his hand. She paused, looking over his shoulder, and felt a shiver of the nerves as she recognised the arrogant dark face he was drawing.

"Is it like?" Sam asked without looking up.

"Very," she said, offhandedly.

He leaned back, smiling at her so that his face was inverted and unfamiliar.

"What did he want? Or was it just a cover for wolfish advances? Did he offer you a pad in Monte Carlo? Or a mink coat with diamond buttons?"

"Fool," she said, flushing. "He wanted you and me to visit their home during the Easter holidays."

"Wow!" yelled Sam, throwing up his charcoal and catching it. "Kianthos! Sounds great."

"I told him I couldn't go, of course," she said, pouring herself some cocoa and sitting down at the table.

Sam looked at her closely. "Couldn't? Or wouldn't?"

"You know I've fixed my holiday," she answered. "I'm going with Peter to this Anglo-Saxon burial site."

"Peter was round this evening," Sam said, irrelevantly. "He wanted to borrow some glue. He made like a gundog after a pheasant when I mentioned Kianthos—seems there's an early Mycenean temple there that has never been properly excavated. The Lillitos family own the whole island and they won't let strangers land."

"Typical!" exploded Kate. "What right do they have to prevent people from seeing a thing like that, an important historical site. . . ."

"Keep your wig on," Sam advised with kindly superiority. "You know, I bet if you mentioned this idea of going there for Easter to Peter he'd jump at it. He would really love to see that temple."

She drew a quick breath. He was right. Peter would certainly want to go there.

Sam yawned. "I'm off to bed now. Goodnight, Sis."

When he had gone Kate sat staring at the charcoal drawing he had made. It really was very like Marc Lillitos.

Some obscure, buried instinct warned her against seeing too much of that man. They were like people from different planets. Their lives had touched by chance, and he had already had a disturbing effect upon her. Her life had been running smoothly for the past year. She had buried the yearning for a musical career, had settled down quietly at home, teaching and planning her life with Peter. And now, in one day, the smooth threads of her life were tangled and knotted.

She picked up the pad and tore the sketch off, holding it up to the light. The arrogant face seemed to smile at her. Angrily she crunched it into a ball and flung it across the room, then went up to bed.

She decided, guiltily, not to mention the projected visit to Kianthos to Peter. She had never practised deceit before, even by omission, and it upset her. But the thought of spending two weeks with Marc Lillitos disturbed her even more.

She was abstracted and dreamy at school next day. Even Pallas, during her daily singing lesson, commented upon it, teasingly. Kate was relieved to find the girl still friendly, and decided that perhaps Marc had not spoken to her of his idea for the holiday, after all.

When she reached home that evening she was in a more cheerful mood. She flung her coat over its hook and walked into the kitchen where, to her amazement, she found Peter and Marc Lillitos seated at the kitchen table, eating hot buttered scones.

There was something so odd about seeing Marc in that homely setting that her lips twitched with unguarded amusement, and, looking back at her, his grey eyes smiled in response. She looked away at once, thinking that it was irritating, the way he read her mind so easily.

"Hi, Kate!" Peter leaned back, offering his cheek, and she bent and kissed him, deliberately, on his mouth. He looked rather surprised, but accepted it calmly.

Mrs. Caulfield was getting another batch of scones out of the oven and Kate exchanged a wry, enquiring glance with her, but her mother only smiled and shook her head, as though totally at a loss to explain the presence of the two men.

Peter took another scone, and said, through a buttery mouthful, "I'd be eternally grateful, Lillitos. I've wanted to see that temple for years. I understand some of it is still standing in situ."

"Yes, it is partially restored," Marc said calmly, his gaze on Kate's flushed and angry face.

"I can't wait to see it," Peter said excitedly. "I could map out the general area of the site, then a full team could come in and do the serious work. I wouldn't disturb the site at all. Just work around,

38

determining the limits of the building, if I could, and estimating the size of team needed for the job."

"Then that is settled," Marc said, still watching Kate with bland amusement.

"Peter!" Kate began, in a quiet voice. "We're going to Sussex for Easter."

He looked vaguely at her. "Oh, that doesn't matter! There'll be plenty of other workers there. But Kianthos—what a chance! I'll be in on the ground floor with this one. I'll get in touch with various people tonight, get them interested. . . ."

"I think that that should wait," said Marc firmly. "I would prefer you to keep the whole thing to yourself until you've seen the temple. Then we can discuss it in the light of what you decide should be done."

"Right," said Peter amiably. "It might be better to have a definite plan in hand." He jumped up, wiping his buttery fingers on his handkerchief. "I'll be off now. I want to do some research on the temple." He offered Marc his hand. "Thanks very much. I am really grateful for this chance."

Kate looked at him, seething, and, suddenly noticing her again, Peter lightly kissed her cheek. "See you, sweetie," he observed vaguely. Then he was gone, banging the front door behind him.

Unable to trust herself to speak, Kate went into the sitting-room where she flung herself down into a chair and brooded furiously. She might have guessed that Marc Lillitos would get his own way. She could cheerfully have strangled Peter at that moment. All he thought of was broken pots and ancient bones. He didn't care that she was in emotional danger from this tank masquerading as a man!

The door opened again, and the human tank came in, and stood, watching her.

She glared at him. "Well, you've got what you wanted. Now go away!"

He flipped his eyebrow. "Have I?" he retorted mockingly. "Do you know what I want, I wonder?"

She did not stop to examine this question too closely, but replied to it as though it were quite straightforward. "You wanted us to come to Kianthos. We're coming. You always get what you want, I suppose?"

He grinned, his hands in his pockets lazily. "Quite often. I am taking the night flight to Greece, but I will see you at Kianthos in two weeks. Give my regards to Sam." He smiled again and left.

Kate walked restlessly round the familiar room, feeling most unfamiliar to herself.

It was ridiculous to be so nervous about a fortnight's holiday. She loved Peter, didn't she? Of course she did. So why should she be anxious about spending time with Marc Lillitos?

I'm behaving irrationally, she told herself crossly. The truth is that I've been influenced by the aura of glamour which surrounds him. He's rich, good-looking, charming, and I've never met anyone like him before. But those are surface things. Underneath I'm still the same person. I still feel as I always did about Peter.

She halted, staring out of the window. A blackbird was singing his evening challenge from the top of the garden shed. The lilac trees were already showing fat green buds. It would soon be full spring. Daffodils were breaking out of their sheaths into frilly yellow under the hedge and there was a flurry of pink blossom on the almond trees in the next garden.

She looked out for a long time, her face absorbed. It was all very real, very beautiful, very reassuring.

Of course I love Peter, she thought, with a surge of relief. She thought of him with warmth. He was a darling—absent-minded, thoughtless, vague—but basically kind and generous if only one could penetrate the mists of antiquity which filled his brain. He might not be dynamic or dangerously attractive, but he was real. She knew him, understood him and cared about him.

She swung on her heel and walked out of the room, mentally snapping her fingers at Marc Lillitos.

CHAPTER THREE

AS the plane landed on the small airfield at Kianthos Kate peered nervously out of the window, wondering if Marc were waiting for them, but there was no sign of him as they climbed down into clear, cool sunlight.

She and Pallas had gone shopping together a few days before they were due to leave, and had returned laden with bags and parcels. Kate had felt guilty, squandering money on clothes for herself, but her mother had firmly insisted that she renew her wardrobe. "Think of yourself for once," she smiled, patting Kate's cheek. "You've done so much for us all since you started work. I don't know what I would have done without you. But it's time you had some really nice clothes."

Kate had suggested she made what she needed, as she normally did, but Mrs. Caulfield had shaken her head.

"No, dear. You may never have the chance of a holiday like this again. Buy them."

Kate was a competent needlewoman, but she had to admit, as she gazed at diminutive bikinis and smart, multi-hued trousers, that she could never have produced anything half as professional.

Pallas was chattering to Sam, as they walked towards the sleek black car which had come to meet them, and Kate had time to look around her.

The airfield ran along beside the beach, the only

flat part of the island, as far as she could see. Above it rose green hills and rugged crags of stone, their peaks swathed in a lavender mist shot through with pink.

A man approached them, taking the bags from the airport manager while saluting Pallas with a grin. The airport manager slid away politely and began locking up the one building visible, a small modern pavilion built of wood.

"Hallo, Jake," Pallas greeted the newcomer. "How are you?"

"Fine, Miss Pallas, just fine." He was a rugged Greek of middle years, with swarthy skin and a broken nose which gave him a slightly pugnacious expression. Stowing their bags into the boot of the car, he helped Pallas into the back.

All the details of the journey had been handled by the Lillitos family. Kate felt quite dazed as she sat back on the smooth upholstery of the limousine, next to Pallas, staring out of the window. Everything had been so trouble-free that she almost doubted that she had really left England. Money certainly oiled the wheels when one was travelling.

"How is my mother, Jake?" Pallas asked, leaning forward.

The driver turned his head to smile reassuringly at her. "Oh, she's okay! Just dandy, Miss Pallas—you know she always gets better in the spring!"

Pallas looked relieved and sat back with a sigh. The car glided along the beach, on a winding road, and mounted beneath dark cypress trees. Below them the airfield spread out like a green handkerchief beside the beach, and the air was filled with a fresh, salty tang.

43

"Is it far to your home?" Sam asked. He was rather pale. Kate suspected that the flight had left him feeling a little sick, but he had not mentioned it.

"A ten-minute drive," Pallas told him. "Our house is at the top of a cove, but we have to go up before we can reach it, as the cliffs cut it off from the airfield. My brother intended to build a large hotel near the airfield, but he hasn't got round to it yet. We don't really want strangers on Kianthos at all." She was looking rather strained herself, today, and Kate guessed that she was nervous about the family reaction when she got home.

"Will it be just your mother and your brother who are at home?" she asked her.

Pallas shrugged. "Perhaps, but then Hélène might be there—she often comes for Easter, with some friends. Or Marc may have business friends of his at the villa. He uses it often, you see, to put them into a good mood before concluding a deal."

"Nice work if you can get it," Sam said, a little gruffly.

Pallas flushed and looked hurt, but Kate could see that her brother was feeling worse with each minute of the journey. His freckles stood out on his nose like micro-dots under a microscope. His mouth was thinned and taut and his cheeks white. She hoped he would not be sick before they reached the villa.

But at that moment the car lurched downwards again, throwing Peter against the door. He rubbed his forehead resentfully, then bent to pick up the vast tome he had been reading ever since they left London. Kate watched him crossly. He had not spoken to any of them all morning. She knew that dreamy, abstrac-

ted expression. It meant that he was unaware of any·
thing around him. Including her.

They stopped in a gully between dark rocky cliffs,
grass clinging perilously to little clefts, wild yellow
flowers blowing in the sea wind. The path was rough
with lumps of stone, but the car reversed slowly,
wheels churning up pebbles, and turned down a
grassy track which ended on a paved patio.

Kate got out and stood with Sam and Peter, like
herded sheep, gazing in amazement at the view spread
before them.

The Villa Lillitos was modern, but built on classical
lines, a two-storey house, with flat, wide windows, a
terrace running along the front on which stood basket
chairs and several small tables. The terrace was sup·
ported on smooth white pillars of stone, and in the
centre of it stood a portico, beneath which Marc
Lillitos stood watching their arrival.

It reminded Kate of a colonial American house,
somewhere in the deep South, and the shady cypresses
which surrounded it did nothing to dispel the illusion
The house stood on a sloping hill, below it a rough
path which presumably led to the sea, for she could
glimpse golden sands and curling blue waves some
way below them. Behind the house she could see
green lawns, spring flowers and the nets of a tennis
court.

Before she had time to take more in, Marc was
with them, giving a quiet order to the driver, taking
Pallas's elbow.

"I am sure you would all like to rest before dinner,"
he said, politely smiling.

A short woman with smooth olive skin, dark hair

45

and black eyes met them in the entrance hall and took charge of the visitors.

Peter hung back and Kate heard him say eagerly, "How soon can I see the temple, do you think?"

She did not wait to hear Marc's reply. Cross and flushed, she went up behind Sam to the room prepared for her.

"My name is Sophia," said the maid politely. "Please do not hesitate to ask me for anything you need." Her English was so good that Kate was quite taken aback. She had been wishing that she had had time to learn some Greek before her trip, but it was becoming clear that she was unlikely to need it. Everyone in the Lillitos household seemed to speak very good English.

She hesitantly tried out one of her few hastily learnt phrases, *"Efharisto!"* which meant thank you.

Sophia smiled, with sudden real warmth, and spoke in reply, in her own language.

Kate flushed. "I'm afraid that's almost the whole of my Greek vocabulary!"

Sophia laughed. "You will learn more, yes?"

"I hope I shall," said Kate. "I would like to be able to speak Greek. I only speak French, and a little German."

"I speak fluent English," Sophia said proudly. "Marc taught me to speak it! I was his nurse. He learnt at school, and I learn from him."

Kate stared in amazement. "His nurse? But you can't be old enough!" Then she flushed. "Oh, I'm sorry, I didn't mean to be rude."

Sophia was not at all cross, though. She beamed, "Why rude? It is very big compliment. I was four-

46

teen when I first come to work for the family. Marc was little baby, just born. I help the nurse, then nurse leave when Marc is two, and I carry on." She looked wistful. "He was very pretty baby. When he was eight, he went away to school. I stayed on as maid." She counted on her fingers, muttering under her breath. "You guess? I am forty-five now."

"You don't look it," Kate said sincerely. "Your complexion is so good!"

Sophia smiled, very pleased, and after another moment or two went off, leaving Kate to change for dinner. She slipped into her new dressing-gown and lay down on the bed for a while. The flight had been more tiring than she had expected. Half an hour later she got up and put on a turquoise dress which she had bought in Greyford. Then she went downstairs and found Peter and Marc in a wood-panelled lounge, talking quietly.

She stood by the door, watching them, feeling a surge of resentment against Marc Lillitos for the bored expression on his dark face. She forgot the number of times she had been irritated by Peter's passion for the past. It never entered his head that not everyone shared his interest, and even Sam had been known to ask him to shut up about ancient civilisation. But now it was just another crime to chalk up against the name of Lillitos, and she illogically felt pleased to be able to do so.

Marc turned his head and saw her. Her heart did that annoying backward flip which she had only begun to notice since meeting him. There was something about the look in the grey eyes which bothered her a good deal—a lazy, mocking intimacy, as though he not only knew and understood her, but could read her mind with a glance. It was alarming to feel so transparent.

She came forward and Peter turned to smile at her. "Oh, there you are, Kate! I've made all the arrangements with Lillitos. He's kindly offered me camping equipment—a tent, blankets, sleeping bag, even cooking facilities."

"You're going to sleep on the site?" Kate interrupted. "But, Peter, this is a holiday!"

He stared, in mild bewilderment. "Well, I couldn't make the journey every day, you know, there and back. The temple is up there," pointing out of the long window, which looked up at a green expanse of mountainous country, "on that hooked peak. Mr. Lillitos says you can see the whole of the island from the top—a good strategic position for a fortress. There must be more than a temple up there." His face glowed passionately. "Who knows what I'll find?"

"You're going to leave me here and spend the whole fortnight alone on that mountain?" she asked incredulously.

"You'll have Pallas and Sam to keep you company," he answered vaguely. "I thought the idea was that you should have fun with Pallas while I work on the site? You know you're never very keen on site work, Kate."

Angrily conscious of Marc's amused gaze, she was silent, and Peter took her agreement for granted. "Well, I'm very grateful," he told Marc. "I'll be off now, then." He shook hands with him, kissed Kate absently and was gone before she had time to think.

She looked at Marc coldly. He was leaning back in his chair, his face sardonic.

"You do not look too happy, Miss Caulfield. Your fiancé will be quite safe, I promise you. My car is taking him as far as the road goes. We do not have too many roads on Kianthos. Jake will help him carry up the camping equipment, and see the camp set up. He has plenty of food with him. And the goatherds will visit the Peak once a day, as they always do, with their goats. If anything went wrong, they would let me know."

"Goatherds?" she asked curiously.

"There's a village on the other side of the peak. They keep goats and have some olive trees. Cheese and olives are the staple diet, you know. Goat's cheese and goat's milk, and fish, in season. They call the peak To Angkistri. It means The Hook. There is a local legend about it which I must tell you some time."

"How long have your family lived here?" she asked.

"Off and on for generations, I believe. My great-grandfather was a fisherman who left the island for the mainland when there was bad fishing for several years. My grandfather was successful enough to build up a good business and my father bought the island thirty years ago. He built this house."

"Sophia said you learnt your English at school," she said. "Was that in England?"

He nodded. "My mother is French, but English schools are famous all over the world, so they decided to send me to England, and then to a French university."

She was startled. "Oh, you were at university?"

His dark face was suddenly alight with laughter. "That surprises you? You thought I was illiterate, I suppose?"

Kate flushed. "I hadn't thought about it," she said offhandedly.

"Well, I left without taking a degree, in fact, because my father was ill, and I had to take over the business. Then he died, so I carried on. I have often regretted it, but that's fate!"

She watched him curiously. His face had a fatalistic look as he said the last words. "Do you believe that?"

His brows rose. "In fate? Of course." His tone was suddenly brusque, as though he disliked the subject.

"Why have you never allowed anyone to visit the temple before?" she asked him after a long silence.

"My father would never have strangers on Kianthos. He felt that they would spoil it. There are so few roads that it would be impossible to bring many cars here, anyway, and modern tourists love to go everywhere by car. The life of our people would change if we allowed too many outsiders on to the island."

"It's such a beautiful place," she said. "Isn't that a selfish attitude?"

"The villagers all agree with me. They are happy as they are."

"Are they? Living on goat's cheese and olives, with occasionally a little fish?"

"Does the technological society make men any happier?" he countered coolly.

"I think your attitude is too possessive," she said.

His eyes flashed across the room at her and she felt

oddly breathless, as though he had touched her. "But I am possessive," he said softly. "Any man worth his salt must be—the desire to possess is the root of love."

She was angrily aware of a weakness spreading through her body, a trembling and fluttering of the nerves. "That's a very old-fashioned idea," she said, trying to laugh, but too conscious of his masculine presence to be able to carry it off. "Nowadays we believe that to love is to be ready to let go. People have to be free."

"Hence divorce?" he said sarcastically. "And the high abortion rate in your country, not to mention the appalling tragedies of drug addiction."

She was grateful when, at that moment, Sam and Pallas came into the room. Sam was still very pale, but the blue line around his mouth had vanished, and some of his normal cheerfulness had returned.

"I am afraid you will not meet my mother this evening," Marc said to him. "She has a headache. But I hope she will get up for lunch tomorrow." He looked sharply at Sam's face. "You look ill. Was it a bad flight?"

Sam grimaced. "I'm the world's worst traveller. Don't worry, though, I'll be fine now I'm back on terra firma."

They dined quietly, in a very modern room with mosaic tiling on the floor and pleasant, yellow walls. Kate ate steak and salad, followed by a very sweet dessert made of figs and cream, after which black coffee seemed very appropriate.

Sam excused himself early, pleading a headache, and Pallas went up to sit and talk to her mother for a while. Kate was intending to go to bed early, too, but Marc said that she would feel more like sleep when she had walked around the garden for a while.

"The air is so pure here," he said, draping her cardigan around her shoulders, his fingers lingering on the nape of her neck for a second longer than was necessary. She shivered at his touch, and he glanced down at her, grey eyes narrowed.

They walked round the garden without talking, listening to the cicadas and feeling the cool dusk stealing over the trees and flowers. The air was, as he had said, fresh and sweet, with a faint scent of spring permeating it. One tree was covered with purple flowers which Marc said were called Judas flowers. High up on the hills the mountain furze was in golden bloom and a final shaft from the setting sun made the slopes glow like molten gold, then the light died and a purple shadow crept over them.

She was reminded of Peter and felt a pang of disloyalty. He had only been gone a short time and already she was forgetting she was engaged to him. Marc was far too experienced in the small art of flirtation for her. She was not sure whether he was deliberately flirting with her, or if it was merely a reflex action, but from time to time she was aware that he was deliberately testing her reactions to him.

Perhaps he had been piqued by her attitude from their first meeting? Or perhaps he liked to have a row of scalps dangling from his belt?

Whatever the reason, those charming smiles, the light, meaning phrases and the way he touched her neck just now—they all added up to a flirtation. And she did not mean to get involved in that sort of folly.

"I think I'll go in now," she said, as they approached the terrace again.

"I'm not in the least tired," he said. "Are you really sleepy? You don't look it. Won't you play for me first? Something quiet and gentle?"

She played a piece of soft night music, by Mozart, and the insidious intricacies gradually drove out all disquieting thoughts from her head, and restored her sense of humour.

I'm a fool, she thought, her fingers moving delicately over the keys. Peter leaves me too much alone. I'm making mountains out of molehills, building ridiculous fantasies. Marc is just being polite. I must get it into proportion.

When she lifted her hands finally and sat back, Marc smiled at her. "You have a very pleasant touch."

"I'm a competent amateur," she said firmly, "but thank you."

He looked at her for a long moment, his face inscrutable. "What a girl for laying out the facts you are," he said at last. "You are unusually honest. I know many much less talented musicians who would claim a great deal more than competence."

She refused to be drawn, smiled and said goodnight, leaving him alone in the lounge.

She was up early next morning and met Sam on the stairs. He looked his usual self once more, cleareyed and alert. He grinned at her, "I slept like a log! How about you?"

"Fine," she admitted.

They found themselves the first to arrive for breakfast. A pretty girl in a lavender overall was moving about, laying the table, and looked round in surprise as they entered the room. She smiled, though, and said good morning in rather thickly accented English, then pointed out the food, waiting over steel hotplates.

There were scrambled eggs, bacon and sausages, but Kate stuck to her usual orange juice and slice of toast. Sam, however, greedily heaped his plate with a glorious mixture of everything, and grinned at her teasingly as he began to eat.

"I heard you playing the piano last night," he said, between mouthfuls.

"Did it wake you? I'm sorry. Marc asked me to play something before I went to bed."

Sam shook his head. "It was quite pleasant, drifting off to sleep to Mozart." He shot her an acute glance. "Don't fall for Marc, will you? He's an attractive sort of chap, but Pallas says he has a girl-friend. French, apparently—a successful model. She won't give up her career or Pallas thinks they would be married by now."

Kate gritted her teeth and spoke very brightly. "A tough career girl should suit him! I hope she keeps him tied up in knots for years. His attitude to women is as out of date as crinolines."

Sam laughed. "You're so right! Look, you don't mind my giving you the gypsy's warning, do you, Sis? It's just that I'd hate you to get hurt."

"You seem to forget I'm engaged to Peter," she said rather sharply.

Sam grimaced. "Yes, but then Peter isn't exactly a ball of fire in the romance stakes, is he? I mean, an Anglo-Saxon kneebone gives him more of a thrill than you do!"

54

"Really, Sam!" she snapped angrily.

Sam looked sheepish. "Oh, I'm sorry. It isn't my business, I know, but much as I like Peter, he does rather neglect you. Girls like a bit of attention from time to time."

"You should write a book on the subject," she said, "as you have so much valuable advice."

Pallas arrived while Sam was groping for a reply, and they dropped the subject. They talked of what they should do that day. The sun was already bright, but cold, and the sky was an unbelievable blue. The idea of a swim that morning was dismissed, and Sam suggested that Pallas show them round the island.

"I wonder how Peter is getting on," said Kate, sipping black coffee slowly.

"Would you like to go up and see?" asked Pallas. "Jake will take you in the car to where the track starts. Would you mind walking the rest of the way, though? It is very tough going."

"Of course I don't mind," Kate said easily. "I've done some hill walking. We went to the Lake District several times for our family holidays. Do you remember, Sam?"

"I remember you puffing and blowing when we got to the top," he teased.

Kate laughed. "Are you sure you don't mind my going off alone, though? It seems very rude. Your brother asked me to come to keep you company, you know. Actually, I would like to make a tour of the island with you—I just felt worried about Peter. . . ."

"I understand," said Pallas, smiling at her. "I'll have Sam to keep me company. Really, I don't mind. You go, and put your mind at rest. I expect you would like to see the temple yourself. Then, when you know how Peter is coping, you can feel free to enjoy yourself with us."

Kate let out a sigh of relief. "Well, thank you, then. I'd like to go."

Pallas came round to the garage with her, to find Jake, and he readily agreed to drive Kate up to To Angkistri. They set out ten minutes later and Jake talked to her all the way. He had, he explained, learnt his English in America.

"My name is Hector Hyakos, but in America they called me Jake for short. The States—a great country. Fifteen years I lived there. Very happy, earn lot of money. But then I met the boss and he says come to Kianthos, be my driver-mechanic-man of work. Handyman, they call it in the States. I figure that I never manage to save enough to come home on my own. So I accept."

"And are you glad you came?" she asked him.

"Sure I'm glad. The boss is a great guy—generous, warm-hearted, a real Greek. And I like cars. I was always homesick, you know? I mean, the States is great, but I'm a Greek." He pulled up with a jolt and she looked around her with great interest. They were on the mountain slope now, the track nothing but a whitened ribbon between grass and rocks, pitted and scarred.

"This is as far as I can take you, miss. You want I should walk up there with you? You follow this track to the top. But it gets difficult as you get higher. You might slip, or get dizzy."

"No, thank you," she smiled. "I have climbed before and I have a good head for heights. You'd better get back—I think Miss Pallas wants you to drive her somewhere."

He saluted. "Okay by me. I'll be back at four o'clock. You got a watch, miss?"

She showed it to him and he nodded. Then he stood by the car, watching her intently as she began the steep climb to the top. After a while he clearly decided she was competent enough, because she heard the sound of the engine, and the grinding of the wheels on stones as he turned back the way they had come.

The climb was more difficult that she had anticipated. Several times she slipped, her hands clutching at the face, but each time she managed to steady herself. She kept going, breathing quickly, her hands scratched and bleeding slightly, her knees and back aching.

When she reached the top she sat down, panting, and stared back the way she had come. From here the climb looked dizzyingly steep, and she wondered how she had had the nerve to attempt it—and also how she was to get down! Then she shrugged. Sufficient unto the day was the evil thereof. . . .

She found Peter lying on his face, stretched flat out, the only part of him which moved his hand, which was delicately scraping at the dusty covering of soil which lay everywhere over the ruins.

He turned his head to squint at her as she approached, and, without a sign of surprise or enquiry, said, "Careful! I've begun marking out the ground plan with string. Don't trip over it or you'll pull out the pegs and I'll have it all to do again."

"You've been busy," she commented, staring around her.

The site was laid out on a flattish plateau, in a vaguely rectangular shape, with three broad stone steps running all the way around the building. The roof had been supported by the usual pillars, some of which still stood, in more or less battered condition, rearing up towards the open blue sky, tapering to their plain capitals, their stone flaking away along the sides. Blocks of stone lay everywhere, among the wiry grass and yellow flowers. It was touching to Kate to see how the stone steps were hollowed out by generations of reverent feet, although this place had been deserted for so long, slowly crumbling under the pressures of wind and weather.

"I only have two weeks to make this preliminary investigation," he pointed out. "Now you're here, Kate, pass me that plastic bag. I've found something interesting."

She ran and picked up the top bag from the pile laid ready, a stone keeping them from blowing away, returned and handed it to Peter, who gently pushed an encrusted object inside the bag.

"That was outside the temple area proper," he said. "Give me my map. Over there. . . ." waving a vague arm.

She fetched the map and Peter carefully marked the spot where he had found his first object.

"What do you think it is?" she asked, staring at it. "A coin?" It was that shape.

He shrugged. "Possibly. We can't tell until it's cleaned." He grinned at her. "It's a temptation to look for other things, but I must get on—until a proper accredited expedition is organised the site mustn't be disturbed. But as the coin was outside the temple that won't matter too much. Now, I want to finish my map today. I'll measure and you can jot down the dimensions."

"Have you had breakfast?" she asked resignedly.

"What?" He stared at her as if she were talking in a foreign tongue, then blinked. "Oh, breakfast. Yes, I had a roll when I first got up."

"At crack of dawn, by the amount of work you've done," she scolded. "What is there for lunch? I'll get you something."

He protested, but she insisted, and at last he gave in, and sat down with her to eat the stew she heated over the little oil-stove. Marc had sent up a number of tins, she found, as well as eggs, cheese and bread. There was no reason why Peter should not eat well.

After lunch they resumed work. They continued to work for the rest of the afternoon, breaking only for a cup of black coffee at two o'clock, and soon had the whole site mapped out. Peter crawled around on his knees, measuring the ground, and Kate carefully marked down the measurements on his rough sketch map. Then they noted down all the positions of pillars, fallen stones and other objects, then measured the pillars, their heights, breadths, capitals.

Kate's shoulders and arms were aching. Her eyes kept blurring and she was hot and weary. But Peter seemed beyond such ordinary human weakness. Frowning, absorbed, intent, he worked on as the sun grew warmer, rose higher and higher, and then began to move down the sky again.

She glanced at her watch and found, to her relief, that it was half past three. She wanted to get back down the peak before Jake arrived, so she said good-bye to Peter, who answered briefly, hardly realising what she had said, she suspected.

Kate was glad to see no sign of the car below. Taking a deep breath, she began to lower herself, clinging to the grassy outcrops of stone, her fingers clawing fiercely, feet feeling for support. She had to climb down backwards. It was impossible to walk down. She was only a short way from the top when she heard the car engine in the distance. It appeared to be racing along the bumpy narrow track. Stones rattled and flew as the wheels spun. She wondered if Jake had intended to get here early to help her down, and then, hearing the car stop with a ferocious jerk, turned her head to smile at him.

The smile froze on her face. It was not Jake, but Marc, who had leapt out of the driving seat of the khaki jeep drawn up far below her.

His expression as he looked up at her was grim. She could see, even from this distance, the tight clenching of his jaw and teeth. The flash of the hard grey eyes.

He was bitterly angry, that much was obvious.

Shock made her move too quickly. She felt her hands slip, felt the tearing pain of the rock biting into her skin, her feet slithering helplessly down. Panic blotted out all thought for an instant, during which time she grasped desperately at the rock face and spreadeagled herself against it, toes curling into the niche they had somehow found.

Stones rattled downwards nearby. She heard quick, harsh breathing. Then an arm clamped round her and she was pulled against a cool blue shirt, her face buried against Marc's chest.

For a second there was a silence, then he asked roughly, "Are you badly hurt?"

Kate lifted her head, without looking up at him, and pushed herself back a little. "No," she whispered. "I'm so sorry...."

She heard his teeth snap together and felt the raging fury inside him, although he said nothing. She felt singed and weary. He was right to be angry with her. She had been silly to attempt the climb.

"Do you think you can make the rest of the way with my help?" he asked tensely.

"Yes," she whispered.

Slowly, inch by painful inch, they descended. She felt his arm tensed permanently to grab her if she fell again, and dreaded the interview that must take place at the foot.

Then, at last, they stood upright beside the jeep. Marc opened the door without looking at her and she wearily tumbled into the passenger seat. He slammed the door and walked round to the other side, got in and then sat staring at her, his arm along the seat.

"You stupid little fool!" he said harshly. "Were you mad to attempt that climb? I thought you were out exploring with Pallas and Sam. It was only when Jake got back that I discovered the truth, and I tore the skin off his back for letting you go up there alone. I drove here like a maniac, expecting to find you in pieces at the foot, only to see you stuck up there, like a fledgling bird.' He glared at her with burning ferocity. "If you weren't in such a state already I would gladly teach you a lesson you won't forget! Never try that climb again. Do you hear?"

She nodded, silenced for once.

"Show me your hands," he commanded, after a long pause.

Trembling, she turned them palm up, and heard his breath drawn in explosively. "Good God!" he exclaimed. They were scraped and bloody, one deep gash at the base of her thumb, grass stains on the raw fingers.

"I wanted to see that Peter was comfortable," she muttered nervously.

"And I suppose he had you working wth him up there?" he asked tautly. "Digging and scraping like a mole all day? Why didn't he see you safely down to the car? He must realise how dangerous that climb can be—or doesn't he care?"

"He was very busy," she said. "If I'd asked him to come with me he would have done, but I didn't ask. . . ."

"He's a selfish, irresponsible idiot!" Marc commented savagely. "No decent man would let his woman make a climb like that!"

"I'm not his woman," she snapped back, "I'm his fiancée. But the relationship is one of shared independence, not slavery! He's not a cave man, and I'm not in need of protection."

His grey eyes stormed at her furiously, the handsome features suddenly rigid and dangerous. "You make love sound like mild friendship. Is that all there is between you two? That isn't love as I know it!"

Something twisted inside her, she lowered her eyes. "I'm sure it isn't," she said in a brittle voice.

His hands grabbed her shoulders, the curled fingers biting into her. For a second she was frozen with panic, then he released her with a thickly drawn breath, turned, and started the engine.

CHAPTER FOUR

THEY made the return journey in less than half the
time Jake had taken, tearing round corners and over
bumps in the road, jolting and swaying furiously. She
clung to her seat, eyes shut, aware of Marc's anger
through every nerve in her body.

When they pulled up outside the villa Sam and
Pallas, who had been sitting on the verandah, rose
nervously and came down to meet them.

Marc ignored them both, helping Kate out of the
jeep with impersonal firmness. She shot a glance up
at him and found his face under a tight control
again, but the grey eyes met hers with the glacial
expression she always found so terrifying.

"Oh, your poor hands!" exclaimed Pallas, catching
sight of them. "What have you done to yourself?"

Marc propelled Kate towards the building, his
hand clamped on her elbow, taking no notice of his
sister. He pushed her upstairs and into the large,
luxurious bathroom.

"Sit down," he ordered, and left her alone for a
moment, returning with a large bottle of iodine and
some plasters. He ran warm water into the bowl, im-
mersed her hands with the gentleness of a trained
nurse, carefully washed and dried them, then anointed
the grazes with iodine, while he put a plaster over the
deeper cut.

Kate held her breath until the iodine had stopped

stinging. "Thank you," she whispered, her blue eyes damp with tears.

He leaned over her, very tall and overwhelming, his eyes on her face.

"Did it hurt badly?"

She forced a wavering smile. "No, not at all."

"You're crying!" He somehow made that sound like an accusation and she felt, again, anger in him.

"I got some dust in my eyes on the road," she said quickly.

He washed her face delicately, wiping her eyes with wisps of cotton wool. She felt like a child again, sheltered, cherished, vulnerable. Why was it so pleasant to have one's face washed for one? she thought vaguely, enjoying the sensation.

He took her chin in his long fingers and turned her face up to him. The savagery she had felt in him had all gone now. A warm indulgence lay in his eyes.

"What a silly child you are," he murmured, smiling quizzically. "You looked like a little girl, with your eyes screwed up tight, and your lip between your teeth. How do your hands feel now?"

"Much better, thank you," she said, very pink. In a way, he was more dangerous in this mood.

He lifted them in his and then bent suddenly and kissed them briefly. They quivered in his grip, then were pulled away.

He straightened, still smiling. "What else does one do with a hurt child but kiss it better?" he teased.

She turned blindly and stumbled out of the bathroom. In a moment she was in her own room, the door safely shut. She leaned against the door, heart pounding.

I mustn't let him get under my skin like this, she thought, eyes tight shut. He's only playing some game or other. I must keep my defences in place. I must hold on to my love for Peter.

That evening, when she came down for dinner, she found Marc in the lounge with a small, slender woman of fifty or so, whose thick black hair, dark eyes and elegant clothes had the mark of the Parisian.

Marc glanced up, smiling. "Ah, here is Miss Caulfield now, Mama." He stood up. "Miss Caulfield, this is my mother."

Mrs. Lillitos smilingly held out a thin hand. "I am so pleased to meet you. Pallas has written to me of you so often that I feel I know you very well. But I cannot think of you as Miss Caulfield—will you let me call you Kate? Such a nice name. It always reminds me of Shakespeare."

Marc broke in teasingly, "Ah, yes—Henry the Fifth! What does he say: There is witchcraft in your lips, Kate. . . ." His eyes provoked her openly, and Kate knew herself to be flushing.

His mother looked round at him, one delicate dark brow lifted in enquiry. "Marc! You must not be so teasing!"

He laughed. "Or did you mean Kate from *The Taming of the Shrew*, Mama? Kate, the prettiest Kate in Christendom, sometimes Kate the curst?"

Mrs. Lillitos clicked her tongue. "That was not very polite, my son. I am surprised at you. Kate is covered with embarrassment. Say you are sorry at once!"

"Ah, Mama," he said lightly, "English girls are

not brought up like our girls, to blush at everything! If Kate is pink it is because she wants to slap me, not because she is shy."

His mother looked from one to the other of them, very slowly. A smile pulled at her lips. "Is that so?" she asked quietly. "I see."

"The first time we met," he went on gaily, "she spat at me like a cross kitten with its back arched. She almost stepped under my car, yet she flew at me furiously for daring to criticise her!"

Watching him from under lowered lashes, Kate suspected his light tone hid resentment. It was the first time had had ever referred to their first encounter.

"Perhaps you were rude to her, Marc," his mother said mildly. "Was he, Kate?"

Kate looked at her and was relieved to see that she was smiling warmly. "Very rude," she agreed, smiling back.

"Ye gods!" he exclaimed. "I was the very model of restraint! And when we met again she tore my character into strips, told me how to run my life and threw me out of her home as if I were a burglar!"

Mrs. Lillitos laughed softly. "The more I hear of her the more I admire her! Now, Marc, go away, and let me talk to Kate alone for a while. You are too disturbing."

He made a violent grimace, but did not argue. When he had gone, his mother smiled at her. "He was, even as a boy—it was like having a hurricane permanently in the house."

Kate laughed. "I can imagine!"

Mrs. Lillitos leaned back. "Tell me about yourself, my dear. Do you like teaching music?"

"I like teaching anyone as talented as Pallas," she said frankly. "It's a great pleasure to feel that one is able to help someone with her gifts."

Mrs. Lillitos did not reply directly. After a pause she said, "And yourself? Are you musically talented? Did you ever want to be a professional pianist?"

"How did you know I was a pianist?" Kate asked in surprise.

"I heard you playing to my son last night. It was very pleasant. You must play for me again some time. Did you enjoy exploring the island today?"

Kate blinked. "I . . . I didn't go with Pallas and Sam," she said slowly. "I went to the temple."

"To Angkistri?" repeated Mrs. Lillitos. "Are you interested in archaeology? We have a young man here now, studying the temple."

"He is my fiancé," Kate explained, smiling in surprise. Why hadn't Marc told his mother that she and Peter were engaged?

Mrs. Lillitos stiffened and stared at her. "Fiancé?" she repeated. "Fiancé?"

Kate would have thought she did not know the word, but she remembered that Mrs. Lillitos was French and must be perfectly familiar with it.

"Didn't Marc tell you?" she asked. "Surely Pallas must have mentioned it to you?"

Then she saw that Mrs. Lillitos was very pale. Her frail hand was groping for the stick which stood propped against her chair.

Feebly she stood up, refusing Kate's offer of help with a silent shake of the head.

"I do not feel very hungry tonight," she said. "I

think I will go back to my room. Will you call my son?"

Kate obeyed and Marc came in quickly, looking at his mother with natural anxiety.

"Give me your arm, my son," she said heavily.

He moved to her side at once and they left the room slowly. Kate sank back into her own chair, baffled. Why had Mrs. Lillitos suddenly altered? Was it just that she had begun to feel ill, or had something Kate said upset her?

Before she could think too closely about it, Pallas and Sam had come in together, talking loudly.

"Oh, you're alone," said Pallas, with obvious relief. "I thought Marc might be in here. Heavens, Kate, if you had seen his face when he discovered we had let you go up to To Angkistri alone! He practically burst a blood vessel. Marc has such set ideas about women. He likes to wrap them in cotton wool for safe keeping." She grinned at Sam. "Although these days he does seem to be making an effort to turn a blind eye to my new clothes and hairstyle. So perhaps he is improving."

"He's a throwback to the knights of old," Sam teased. "His recipe for life starts, first catch your damsel. . . ."

Pallas giggled. "Club her," she suggested, "and throw her over your horse."

Sam played up. "Gallop away with her to your castle," he added, twirling an imaginary moustache, "and shut her up in an ivory tower." He sighed exaggeratedly. "Ah, those were the days!"

"Nowadays," said Marc's cool tones from the door, making them all look round guiltily, "your knight

69

would have a hard time telling the damsels from the other young men."

"But think what fun he would have trying to find out!" Sam countered impudently.

Marc's brows rose. "Really? Shall we go in to dinner now? Mama does not feel well enough to stay down, Pallas. She has one of her headaches."

They had moussaka for dinner—aubergines thinly sliced, rich dark minced lamb and a thick cheese sauce covering it all. Kate enjoyed it very much and determined to make it when she got home.

Marc peeled an apple slowly, his long slim fingers deft in all their movements. Kate watched him, remembering the gentleness of those fingers on her face earlier.

"By the way, Pallas, Hélène cabled today. She arrives at the end of the week," he said without looking up.

His sister looked up, frowning. "Alone?"

He shook his head and shot her a quick glance. "She is bringing Marie-Louise and Jean-Paul with her."

Pallas dropped the fork with which she was eating a confection of chocolate and cream. "Jean-Paul?" she repeated breathlessly. "Oh, why did you have to invite him here?"

"Why shouldn't he come here?" Marc demanded. "He is our cousin, after all. And he usually visits us once a year."

She pushed back her chair, standing up suddenly. "It isn't fair!" she wailed, like a child, and ran out of the room.

Sam stared after her, then looked at Marc, who

calmly went on peeling his apple, the rings sliding from between his fingers in symmetrical spirals.

Silently, Sam followed Pallas out of the room. Kate felt curious, yet nervous. She wanted to know why Pallas so much disliked the idea of a visit from this cousin of hers, and yet she was tensely aware of being left alone with Marc once more.

He cut himself a slice of the apple, bit it with relish, and then smilingly offered her half. She shook her head. But before she could ask him about his sister's reaction to his news, he had said lazily, "Did you know that Spiro Pyrakis lived near here?"

She dragged her mind back from the thoughts which had been absorbing it.

"Spiro Pyrakis? No, I didn't. I have all his records at home. He's my favourite pianist. I went to all his London concerts last year, and I found his playing even better than I'd dreamed. Of course, a recording is never the same as the real thing."

"He's a friend of mine," he said casually.

She stared at him, too awed to speak.

"I was talking to him on the telephone this morning," he said lightly. "He asked me to sail over there tomorrow. Would you like to come?"

"I couldn't," she stammered, torn between delight and awe. "He wouldn't want to meet a stranger. . . ."

"I told him about you," Marc went on, "asked if I might bring you. He said it would be delightful to meet a pretty girl." He grinned at her, his grey eyes alight with wicked amusement. "Spiro loves the company of pretty girls and he has been shut up on Epilison for weeks, writing a new concerto. He jumped at you like a hungry trout jumping at a fly."

Kate flushed. "I'm sure he didn't," she protested.

"Wait until you meet him. You'll see I am telling the truth. You'll come?"

"If you're sure . . ." she said nervously. "Are Pallas and Sam going, too?"

"No," he said firmly. "Too many people would irritate him. He hates a crowd."

"Pallas is a pretty girl," she suggested innocently, her eyes on his face.

He grinned at her. "Spiro has known her since she was knee-high to a cicada—he would squabble with her. There is something childlike about him, you know. He and Pallas always quarrel, but they are fond of each other."

Kate excused herself early, pleading fatigue, and he stood at the bottom of the stairs, watching her. "If your back is aching I have some liniment that might help," he offered, seeing her involuntarily holding her back.

She shook her head. "It doesn't matter. Thank you."

"I promise not to kiss the sore place again," he offered teasingly.

Red and furious, she did not answer, but ran quickly up the stairs.

Next morning she was downstairs early for breakfast, wearing blue denim jeans and a loose matching jacket. Her thick, white ribbed sweater gave her a boyish look, emphasised by the fact that she had tied her blonde hair at the back into a ponytail. The severe style gave a new vulnerability to her face, of which she was unaware.

Marc was sitting at the table, eating rolls and dark

red jam. He eyed her lazily. "You look about seventeen," he commented.

Kate took a boiled egg from the silver covered dish and came to sit down opposite him.

He leaned over and teasingly cut a slice of toast into thin strips for her. "Little girls like to have soldiers to dip into their eggs, don't they?"

She gave him a dignified frown. "What time do we leave?" she asked forbiddingly.

He laughed aloud, his mood clearly relaxed and carefree this morning.

They walked down to the small quay a quarter of an hour later. Marc helped her to climb aboard his neat little yacht, cast off and jumped on board himself. The wind took the sails and Kate looked up at them with pleasure as, white and free, they slapped to and fro above her.

"Watch your head," Marc ordered curtly, and she ducked down at once as the beam swung round.

The wind blew behind them all the way to Epilison, the neighbouring island on which Pyrakis lived. They made the crossing in an hour and a half.

The island looked beautiful as they skimmed closer. Blue, shadowy hills, golden sands, white houses, shimmering in the early morning sun, in an unreal beauty which reminded her of a postcard come to life. They tied up at a small jetty and walked up, along narrow village streets, past the untidy white houses whose doors all seemed to stand permanently open. Old women in black sat on some of the doorsteps, shawls over their grey heads, their wrinkled, tanned faces smiling at Marc as he walked past. He paused to speak to each one, gallantly, teasingly, and they giggled at what he said.

Fishermen mending nets waved to him, little boys begged for drachmae. Everyone seemed to know him and like him.

They paused at the very top of the hill and he pushed open high iron gates set in a flinty wall which ran around a charming, untidy garden, set with cypress and gnarled old olive trees.

The house was of an ornate, oriental design, the windows all curves and arches, the stonework fretted. Kate was so nervous that when Marc, with a sharp glance, smiled and held her hand as if she were five years old, she did not protest, but clung to his protection.

"Suppose he's angry because you brought me?" she whispered. "He probably prefers his privacy, like most famous people."

He squeezed her fingers comfortingly. "Goose! I told you, he loves pretty blonde girls!"

She giggled, and then the door opened and a fierce old man, his thick grey moustaches quivering, glared at them from flashing black eyes.

Marc spoke to him, in Greek, grinning affectionately, and the old man answered in a low, grumbling voice, his hands moving in vivid emphasis. Kate saw him shooting those black eyes at her, and looked nervously up at Marc.

He laughed, slipping an arm around her shoulders. "He says he does not like young ladies coming here because Pyrakis always falls madly in love with them, especially when they are blonde and beautiful, like you!" And his grey eyes glinted wickedly.

She blushed and stammered, "I don't believe he said anything of the sort!" She moved away, so that his arm slid off her shoulder.

Marc's eyes continued to laugh at her. He spoke again to the old man, grinning, and the old man laughed, deep in his throat.

He talked gutturally, gesticulating, and Marc laughed. Then they walked into the cool, shadowy hall and the old man shuffled away, his great hooked nose like an eagle's beak, in profile.

Kate stared around her in fascination. The floor of the hall was tiled in black and white marble. A gold-painted tub stood in one corner, full of tall waving ferns, and opposite her hung a gilded mirror in which her own face swam, like a translucent mermaid's, against the dim background of the hall.

"That is Kyril. He has been with Spiro for years and is devoted to him, in a fierce, scornful way. They shout at each other and swear to kill each other, but they are inseparable." Marc came up behind her, staring over her shoulder at her face in the mirror.

Their eyes met. Hers fell away, shyly, at something odd in his. Then Kyril came back and led them down the hall. The room they entered was long, austere and as shadowy as the hall. Beyond open french windows she could see a cluster of bushes and tall cypress, whose branches darkened the room, giving it an undersea look, a cool greeny light filtering through and spilling over books, tables, chairs.

In a shabby old armchair sat Spiro Pyrakis, his leonine head turned towards them.

He rose, holding out his powerful fingers, first to

Kate, "*Mia kiria*," he murmured, his slightly protruding blue eyes appraising her. Then his polite smile widened. "Marc," he said, in charmingly accented English, "you lied to me, you dog!"

Marc raised an enquiring eyebrow.

"You told me she was pretty," said Pyrakis. "She is enchantingly lovely!" And the blue eyes gleamed down on her. She was not so inexperienced that she could not recognise the glance of desired possession, and a hot blush rose to her cheeks.

Marc moved restlessly, but said nothing. Pyrakis raised her fingers, very very slowly, and kissed each one separately, his eyes still fixed on her pink face.

"What innocence, what delicacy!" he murmured. "To see her blush is like seeing a rosebud open."

Marc moved to the window and stood with his back to them, his hands jammed into his pockets.

"She is a pianist, Spiro, and an admirer of yours."

"Of course," purred Pyrakis, smiling. He turned Kate's hands over, inspecting them. "Your fingers told tales to me," he said, softly. "These little tips work hard. Either a typist or a pianist. I suspected a pianist, because of this . . ." and he delicately touched the pulse which beat at the base of her slender throat. "Sensitive, responsive little creature! Ah, if I were younger! To see that tell-tale beat stir at my touch!" He sighed romantically.

Kate looked helplessly at Marc's unresponsive back. "I . . . I teach, Mr. Pyrakis, I'm not an artiste . . ." she stammered, trying to withdraw her hands without seeming rude.

His face relaxed and a great charm flowed out towards her. "A good teacher is the bounty of heaven," he said gently. "I had a wonderful teacher!"

He released her hands and waved her to a chair. Much relieved, she sank into it, and Marc turned round and also took a seat.

Pyrakis glared at the door. "Where is that fellow, that thief, that rascal?" he bellowed in rapid Greek, and from somewhere in the house a loud voice replied in fierce tones.

Soon the old man reappeared, carrying a little table. They sat around it, drinking black coffee and nibbling slices of honey-drenched pastry sprinkled with almonds.

Marc mentioned Pallas and Spiro Pyrakis bared his teeth.

"Has she begun to work yet, the lazy, idle girl?"

"Miss Caulfield is her teacher. Ask her," said Marc lightly, leaning back, his hands on the arms of his chair.

Pyrakis looked at her, one thick brow raised. "What do you think of her?"

"She is beyond me," Kate confessed. "I think she has great promise."

He gestured impatiently. "Of course, but the temperament! She will not work. A musician needs tenacity, humility, stamina. Pallas lacks them all."

"Kate has great confidence in her!" said Marc.

"Kate?" Pyrakis stared at her, his blue eyes caressing. "What a brusque name for such a feminine creature. I would call her . . ." he paused, looking her up and down slowly until she was once more bright pink. "Penelope!" he announced in triumph. "Yes, Penelope. She has that gentle, stubborn look of Homer's Penelope. Prepared to wait until eternity for her man. Fragile, delicate but unbreakable. That is what I like in some blonde Englishwomen—that look about the mouth that puts up the fence against all intruders." He grinned wickedly, at Marc, his eyes acute. "You have seen it, eh? *Oriste?* It is so inviting. How can one resist that cool, sweet mouth? Any more than a little boy can resist the sign which says no walking on the grass, eh?"

Marc did not answer, but his face was set in rigid lines as he stared back at Pyrakis, and the other man lifted his thick black brows slowly, speaking in Greek.

Marc reddened, but did not reply.

Pyrakis turned back to Kate, his expression more serious, and said, "So you have confidence in Pallas? Does she yet care about her work? Does she work hard for you? Does she worry?"

"I think she is so afraid to care that she pretends to be indifferent," said Kate, looking at Marc. "She thinks her family will never let her have a career, anyway."

Pyrakis turned to Marc, enquiringly. "Why does she think that, my friend?"

Marc shrugged. "We told her she would have to prove herself before we agreed. We did not say she could not try."

Pyrakis nodded and looked at Kate again. "You must make her work, little one. Be cruel, be ruthless, but make her work." Then he stood up, flexing his fingers. "Now I shall play to you."

He walked to the great piano which dominated one side of the shadowy room, lifted the lid and laid his hands on the keys, flat, unmoving.

She had seen this odd trick of his before, at London concerts. He said it was because he wanted to feel the piano before he began to play it, to sense the willingness of the keys.

He lifted his hands again and then broke into a series of fast, dizzying chords which startled her and were totally new to her ear.

"This is his own," Marc whispered.

Pyrakis played for an hour, totally absorbed, as though he had forgotten them, his untiring hands wrenching brilliant response from the piano.

When he stopped playing and swung round to face them, Kate was trembling with excitement. She could not speak, but her face spoke for her.

"I must go now, for my siesta," Pyrakis said. "You will lunch with me afterwards?"

"I'm sorry," Marc apologised, "but I have just noticed the sky. A storm is in the offing. We must make a dash for Kianthos, I'm afraid."

Pyrakis shrugged. "A pity, I shall feel deprived. I was looking forward to more of Miss Kate's company. She is excitingly responsive, like a well tuned violin." He kissed her hand, then, saying something in Greek to Marc, bent and kissed her on the mouth.

Marc took her elbow. "We must hurry. I'll see you, Spiro."

He marched her back down to the harbour very fast, his face coolly shuttered, and helped her into the yacht.

They set off at once. Kate looked back at the island, its hills now dark and menacing with the approaching storm.

Then she sighed. She would remember that meeting with Pyrakis all her life.

Marc shouted to her to come and help him, and she hurriedly obeyed.

She had done little sailing before, but she was light on her feet, and quick-witted, so they worked together in comparative harmony.

"I don't like the look of that sky," he said anxiously. "I hope we get back before that wind veers, or we may be blown right off course. I wish I had noticed the sky earlier."

They were within sight of Kianthos when the wind suddenly began to blow strongly, beating them to and fro as if the boat were a matchstick. Kate caught a glimpse of Marc, through a turmoil of whipped spray, and heard him shouting to her, but the wind blew his words away.

Then the boat seemed to fly upwards, like a toy in the grip of a giant, and she was thrown across the deck, cracking her head with such violence that she lay still, her eyes shut, the pain crashing over her unbearably.

CHAPTER FIVE

SHE lay crumpled against the side of the yacht for a moment or two, waiting for the pain to subside. Dimly, she heard Marc shouting anxiously, "Kate, Kate, are you badly hurt?"

She got herself up on one knee, staggering as pain shot through her head, and he bellowed at her to stay down.

"I can manage, but if you go overboard in this sea I shall not be able to do a thing about it!"

They fought their way doggedly, the coast shimmering through mountains of spray, but the wind was driving them off all the time.

They rounded a sheer cliff and Kate gasped in horror as she saw black rocks rising up, their jagged points like broken teeth above the water. Marc was desperately trying to avoid them, but the wind was too strong.

A grinding crash, the sound of splintering wood, and Kate again felt herself thrown about like a rag doll. This time icy water engulfed her. Panic made her strike out furiously, arms flailing. The cold water seemed to be dragging at her, pulling her downwards.

Then Marc swam up at her side, grabbing her by the throat from behind, turning her on to her back in a deft rolling movement.

"Keep quite still," he ordered. "Relax. Let yourself flop, but trust me. . . ."

Panic was choking her as she felt herself, helpless, being towed like a stranded whale, but she forced herself to obey him.

He swam strongly, but she realised how tiring it must be, and when they had passed the black rocks and were nearing the misty shoreline, she called to him to let her swim alone now.

"I can manage," she assured him.

He released her, and she swam beside him until they were in shallow waters.

Panting, shivering, coughing, they lay on the sands, the sea flinging vengeful breakers after them. She heard a booming sound close by, like the breaking of waves, but realised it was her own heart.

Marc turned over on to his side and looked at her. "How do you feel?" he panted.

She laughed breathlessly, "Rotten. My chest is almost bursting after all that exertion."

"Can you walk? There is a goatherd's hut on the cliff. We'll get food and dry clothes there. The path is not as steep as the path at To Angkistri."

Kate flushed, remembering that day, and struggled to her feet. The wind whipped through her wet clothes. She shivered.

Marc was watching her with concern. "Perhaps you ought to wait here," he said.

She felt panic sweeping over her again. "No," she said quickly, "don't leave me here alone. . . ."

His face softened and he held out his hand. "Come on, then."

What, she wondered, as she climbed the cliff path at his side, had happened to her hatred and resentment? From their first meeting she had had a picture of him as an arrogant, overbearing tyrant whose every word put her back up. She had detested his self-assurance, his sarcasm and scornful dismissal of women as mere playthings. When had all that changed?

She flinched away from too close an examination of her new feelings. That she no longer bristled at the sight of him was sufficient food for thought at the moment.

The goatherd's hut was built of warm creamy stone, rough and unfaced, but as solid as the rocks beneath it. The one small window was shuttered and the door closed.

There was no answer to their knock, so Marc pushed the door open and shouted. No reply came. The small room beyond was empty. A wooden ladder led up into the tiny attic bedroom, from which wisps of straw protruded, leading Kate to conclude that it was a hay loft as well as a bedroom.

Marc went out again and walked round the hut, shouting. Then he came back, shrugged. "Nobody in sight. I'll get a fire going. There's an outhouse with plenty of dry wood stacked up." He opened a large wooden cupboard which took up the whole corner by the fireplace and produced a thick oiled wool sweater, which he flung to her, telling her to put it on while he got the wood.

Gladly she slipped out of her wet clothes and into the sweater. It was obviously intended for a huge man, and fell to her knees, the sleeves hanging far below her wrists. But it was comfortingly warm and she huddled into it with gratitude. She rummaged in the cupboard when she was dressed and found a pair of rough trousers and a long white shirt which she thought would fit Marc.

He came back, laden with wood, and grinned at her, his glance running over her sweater and the long bare legs beneath. "You do look a picture," he teased.

She slipped her feet, shuddering, back into her sodden plimsolls, then took her wet clothes outside to hang on the wire line which stretched between two small posts. When she got back Marc had coaxed the fire into life and was standing beside it, in the goatherd's baggy trousers, the shirt in his hand.

She stood at the door, looking at the bare brown shoulders turned towards her. Under the smooth tanned surface of his skin his muscles rippled as he moved. Her breath caught as she felt an insidious warmth deep inside her, and Marc, hearing the little sound, turned quickly.

"You don't mind being alone here with me like this?" he asked, slipping into the shirt.

"Why should I?" she answered offhandedly.

He buttoned the shirt front, staring at her with narrowed eyes. "Some girls might feel . . . threatened . . . being alone with a man in such circumstances. This is a very isolated spot."

She forced a laugh. "I have too much common sense. You've just narrowly escaped drowning, after all. You're cold, tired and hungry. The last thing on your mind is sex, I would say."

He grimaced. "I see," he said on a strange note. "It is just as well you have so much . . . what did you call it? Common sense. Rather uncommon, I would have said. But I would hate to be stuck here with a female who expected rape at any minute."

"What we both need is food," she said lightly. "I wonder where the goatherd keeps it?"

Marc opened a drawer and produced a flat loaf of dark bread, sugar, a tin of anchovies and some goat's cheese in a yellow dish.

"Giorgiou always keeps his food there," he explained, "and there is coffee here..." producing a wooden tub. While Kate sliced the bread on the small, home-made table, he ground the coffee and opened the anchovies.

She toasted the bread, spread it with cheese and anchovies and held it in front of the fire until the anchovies curled slightly, and the cheese bubbled.

They ate the meal by the fire, sitting on low stools. The black coffee was hot and sweet. It ran through her like fire, making her sleepy and content.

"Are we going to try to get back to the villa tonight?" she asked.

Marc shook his head. "We wouldn't make it. The terrain is too difficult. I would not care to try in the dark."

"You would try if you were alone," she guessed.

He shrugged his shoulders. "As that situation does not arise there is no point in discussing it. We must stay here until dawn. Giorgiou is bound to be back then. He is probably visiting his sister in the village." He threw some more wood on the fire and the flames leapt upwards. She watched them, feeling lazy and at ease.

"You can sleep upstairs," Marc told her. "The bed

is only a straw mattress, but you must have some sleep."

She looked at the wooden ladder. Yawning, she got up and went towards it, then heard a distinct scampering above her head.

Marc leapt towards her as she screamed, and she flung herself into his outstretched arms without thinking, clinging to him, shuddering. "Rats! I saw one . . . its tail. . . ." She was almost physically sick, her teeth chattering with repulsion and horror.

He held her tightly, one hand clenched on her shoulder, his thumb moving over her thin-boned shoulder blade. "You're quite safe," he whispered, his mouth just above her hair.

"I hate them," she stammered. "Horrible, creeping things . . ." burying her face in his chest with tightly shut eyes.

"Kate, stop this," he said, in suddenly hardened tones, holding her away from him. "You have been brave up till now. Stop it!"

The shock of his sudden coldness snapped her back to self-awareness. She was scarlet at once, realising what she was doing. "I'm sorry," she said stiffly, and drew away from him, her eyes on the floor.

"I am relieved to see you have some feminine reactions," he said, reverting to his teasing. "For a girl who came so calmly through a violent storm, shrugged off the possibility of rape with the utmost scorn and has been so level-headed and sensible all day—you amaze me! Who would have thought you would jib at rats!"

She could not control the quick shiver which ran over her. "I . . . I don't like them," she said.

86

"Obviously," he nodded. "But they are clever little creatures, you know. I would have expected you to be kinder about them, such animal lovers are the English!"

She saw that he was attempting to put things back on a normal footing, and tried to respond. "They're like some men," she said, lightly, "clever but loathsome!"

He grinned. "Present company excepted, I hope?"

Kate laughed. "Did that come too near home?"

He grimaced. "I'll get some straw and make a bed on the floor."

Within ten minutes they were both lying on warm dry straw, near the hearth, covered by a heap of thick blankets.

The room was dark, except for the glow of the fire, and Kate felt her eyes growing heavy. She could feel every little movement Marc made, hear his regular breathing. How strange, she thought sleepily, to be here like this with him. She giggled at the thought of what Miss Carter would say if she could see them.

"What's funny?" Marc asked softly, turning his head towards her.

She told him, still laughing.

"And your fiancé?" he asked. "Would he be shocked?" He paused, then added, "Jealous, perhaps?"

"Peter? Good heavens, no, why should he be? He trusts me."

Marc was silent for a moment, and she thought he had gone to sleep, but then he spoke again, making her start, his tone sharp and unpleasant.

"Oh, he trusts you, does he? But what about me?

Does he trust me? A stranger of whom he knows nothing?"

She opened her mouth, but how could she bear to let him know that Peter was too absorbed in his work to care what she did?

He waited for her to answer, then said, "You have been engaged for a long time. When do you plan to marry?"

"Oh, some time next year," she said vaguely. "We haven't actually fixed a date."

He spoke abruptly, his voice hard. "When I get married I shall do so with all possible speed. No long engagement for me. I want to be certain of my girl."

Was he thinking of his French girl-friend, the model? "Do you hope to marry soon?" she asked.

He hesitated for several minutes before replying. "It is in my mind," he said slowly, at last. "But there are . . . problems."

"Your girl-friend isn't ready for marriage yet?" she suggested. So he was thinking of the French girl. Kate wondered what she looked like. Very beautiful, suavely dressed and sophisticated, she decided. With hard eyes.

He seemed to be choosing his words very carefully. "There is someone else," he said. "I have a rival!"

She heard the roughness of his tone, and felt a knife twist in her heart. He was jealous of this girl. He must love her very much to reveal his pain to a comparative stranger like this. She forced herself to continue to talk, although she was feeling dull and miserable.

"I'm surprised you allow that," she said teasingly.

"I would have expected you to sweep him away."

"Oh, I would like to," he said harshly. "But I am not sure of her. . . ."

"You're not sure you love her?" she asked involuntarily.

"Oh, I love her," he said, in a deep shaken voice, "more than I thought possible. But it is she who . . ." he paused, taking a deep breath.

"Who can't make up her mind?" she suggested brightly. "I'm sorry." A thought struck her. "She won't mind about us, will she? About us being here, like this, alone?"

He laughed bitterly. "I wish I could believe she did mind. But she would be totally indifferent." He paused, then added contemptuously, "As indifferent as your Peter."

Kate flushed and did not answer. They said nothing more, and she gradually fell asleep.

When she woke she found the fire out, the room cold but filled with cool grey light. Marc had gone, but her clothes, now bone dry, were laid out for her on the little table.

She dressed quickly, shivering a little, and looked down with a grimace at her clothes. They were dry, but needed ironing, and the salt had stiffened them so that they crackled slightly as she moved. A pale sheen covered them, a salt bloom which flaked away as she brushed at it with her hands. It was lucky she had been wearing practical denim, she thought.

She found Marc outside, walking to and fro with his hands in his pockets. He, too, wore his own clothes again. His white towelling shirt and blue jeans were as crumpled as hers, but she felt a quick tug of the heart at the sight of him. It was strange how quickly she had grown accustomed to being with him. There was a dangerous sweetness about being here, alone, with Marc.

"Giorgiou came back two hours ago," he said. "He woke me and I sent him to fetch Jake. He only has an old donkey which wouldn't carry two of us, and it is too far to walk."

"I'll tidy his house for him," she said.

"There's no need," Marc said brusquely. "I will compensate him for everything."

She felt herself going hot. "Money isn't the answer to everything, you know!" she snapped. That unconsidered remark of his somehow brought all her old resentment rushing back. Last night, in their shared danger and discomfort, she had forgotten how wide the gulf between them was, but she remembered now.

Marc gave her a long, hard stare. "Giorgiou will be quite satisfied," he said harshly. "Do you think he would like you to act as an unpaid servant in his house, sweeping and washing? He would be embarrassed and bewildered."

"Who do you think does all the housework in my home? We have no servants. We do it ourselves." She turned towards the house, but he caught her wrist.

She looked down at his long brown hand meaningly. "Let me go!"

His eyes were savagely angry. "You are not going to do any housework while you are on Kianthos! I will not allow it!"

"You? What gives you the right to order me about?" she gasped furiously. "You live in a private

90

dream of your own, but I live in the real world, and a little sweeping and washing up will do me no harm at all."

"It will do me harm," he said forcefully. "You are my guest. I will lose face with my own people if they think I have guests who work like domestic servants."

Kate was almost in tears, yet could not help laughing wildly. "I can't believe it! What a Victorian attitude! You've got to be joking!"

The blare of the car horn made them both jump. Marc dropped her wrist with a contemptuous glare. "There's Jake," he said, and she wondered if she was wrong in fancying there was a note of relief in his voice.

She looked at the little hut, hesitantly. Marc saw her glance and took her by the elbow, propelling her towards the waiting jeep.

"There isn't time now, anyway," he said, with satisfaction.

"I ought to kick your ankle for that!" she hissed, as they marched towards the jeep.

He laughed, with one of his bewildering changes of mood. "Try it, my girl, and see what happens!" He looked down at her. "Your jeans have shrunk a little. I'll get you some new ones. The sea-water always ruins cloth."

She flushed. "There's no need, thank you. Denim is meant to stand up to salt water."

"What a proud, stubborn creature you are!" he murmured. "I am responsible for ruining them, remember? It was my yacht that you were on when you fell in the sea. . . ."

"I'm responsible for myself," she retorted, "and they'll be fine when they have been washed."

Jake greeted them with a broad grin, which disappeared when Marc curtly told him to get a move on back to the villa. "I've some business calls coming through."

The journey passed in total silence. Marc stared out of the window, his profile rigid. She glanced at him under her lashes, wondering what he was thinking about. He looked angry.

She was angry with him. His automatic gesture of money had offended her. Did he think he could buy everything? They had come through threatened death, spent the night alone, eaten a scratch meal, cooked by both of them in harmony, and yet now he spoilt it all by offering to buy her new clothes. It seemed to be an attempt to reduce her to a lower level once more—to make her a subordinate, an employee, one of his small responsibilities.

It stung badly. All right, she thought, he's a millionaire and I'm just a schoolteacher whose salary wouldn't keep him in shoe leather! But I won't stand for a situation in which he is King Cophetua and I'm just the beggarmaid.

She brooded all the way back to the villa, ignoring the rugged scenery through which they passed, the tangled glory of yellow furze, the grey rock and tumbling green slopes. The cool mists rolled away and the sky grew bright, burning blue.

"Going to be a great day," Jake said hopefully as they climbed out of the jeep.

Marc ignored him, but Kate gave him a warm smile. "A lovely morning," she agreed.

Jake shot a wary glance at Marc's back, then winked.

Kate followed Marc up the steps on to the verandah. As he held open the door for her to pass into the house, she looked up with a deliberately cool expression and said, "By the way, we never did fix how much we were to pay you for our holiday. You'll let us know, won't you?"

His face looked first amazed, then black with rage. She felt her nerves leap at the look he gave her. "You little . . ." he began violently, grabbing hold of her shoulders and shaking her.

"Marc! My son, what are you doing? Have you taken leave of your senses, to shake a young girl like that?"

Marc's hands dropped from Kate like stones, and he turned to confront his mother stiffly.

She stared from one to the other of them, frowning, very pale and fragile in a black satin housecoat.

"Well?" she demanded. "What is the matter? Will neither of you tell me?"

"I'm sorry, Mrs. Lillitos," Kate said quietly. "It was my fault, I'm afraid. Marc offended me and I insulted him to . . . to get my own back." The words sounded childish and stupid as she said them, and she flushed hotly.

His mother threw up a protesting hand. "I am at a loss for words! But I am too relieved to see you both to be angry. Come, my son, kiss me!"

Marc obeyed, and she clung to him.

"I hope you were not too anxious, Mama," he said gently. "We were quite safe once we reached land, but I had no means of letting you know."

93

Sam tumbled down the stairs, dressed in a sweater and jeans. "Glad to see you, Sis," he muttered, hugging her clumsily. "We began to think you were in Davy Jones's locker." Then he threw a nervous look at Mrs. Lillitos and bit his lip.

She held out a hand to Kate. "My dear, I hope your holiday has not been totally ruined by such an unpleasant accident. I am so sorry this happened."

Kate smiled, shaking her head. "I'm pretty tough, Mrs. Lillitos. I was frightened at the time, but I'm fine now."

"But there is a bruise on your forehead. How did that happen? It looks very painful."

"I'll ring the doctor," Marc said brusquely.

"There's no need," Kate protested.

He turned on her, his dark face savage. "You'll see him! Even if you pay him yourself!"

There was an astounded silence as he slammed out of the room. Kate forced a laugh, conscious of her burning cheeks.

"I'm afraid he's cross this morning. The boat is a total write-off, you know." She looked at his mother nervously.

Mrs. Lillitos watched her thoughtfully. "Don't worry about it, my dear. Marc is a man of great depths of emotion. He is quickly angry, quickly calm. Next time you see him he will be his usual self, I'm sure."

Kate doubted that. After what she had said to him, Marc would dislike her intensely. His expression had been dangerously violent when he turned on her just now. She had had the impression that he could almost have killed her.

She went to her room, meeting Pallas on the way, had a short chat with her, and then, with relief, had a long, hot bath. She lay soaking in the water, thinking back over the events of the last few hours. She must try to keep her temper. Marc couldn't help treating everything as a commodity to be paid for, could he? It was the way he had grown up, in a mercenary world.

I must see Peter again, she thought. Already the day she had spent with him seemed an eternity ago, as though she had travelled hundreds of miles and changed totally in the meantime.

She must reassure herself. She got out of the bath, dripping wet, and stared at herself in the full length mirror on the wall. She even looked different. She could not be sure what it was, but her eyes had a new expression. They were more alive, more secretive, as though concealing something, even from herself. That look of youth was beginning to go. Her mouth had an adult bitterness in its curves.

She shivered, and began to dry herself vigorously. Slipping into her new dressing-gown, she padded towards her own room, and met Marc coming out of his. He still wore his jeans and sailing shirt. They looked at each other in silence for a moment.

"I've rung the doctor," he said curtly. "He'll be here in four hours. He has to come over from Epilison and this is not his usual day for visiting Kianthos."

Kate shrugged, "There's no hurry." She went past him, in a cloud of perfumed talcum, and he caught her arm.

"Kate," he said huskily, "why do you fight me all the time?"

She couldn't look up at him. She was too painfully aware of him, big and dark and dominating,
standing very close to her. He waited for a moment,
then dropped her arm and stalked away down the
stairs.

He did not appear at lunch, nor did his mother,
who was recovering from the shock of believing them
both drowned yesterday. Sam, Pallas and Kate
lunched quietly together. Then the doctor arrived,
examined her and pronounced her perfectly fit, but
slightly shocked.

"No more excitement," he ordered. "Rest, relaxa-
tion." He spoke little English, but Pallas translated
for him, while also acting as chaperone.

Kate spent the afternoon on the stone patio, with
Sam and Pallas, lying on well-sprung canvas loungers
enjoying the sunshine.

The storm seemed to have blown quite away, leaving the island calm and peaceful. Out of the wind
the air was warm and still. The sun seemed almost
hot on her bare back and legs.

She wore her new bikini, two delicate scraps of
black cotton which emphasised her slender waist. Sam
rubbed sun lotion into her skin, offering to perform
the same task for Pallas.

"My complexion is intended for this climate," she
claimed triumphantly. "The sun is kind to me. I never
use those things."

Kate was very tired this afternoon. Her experiences
of yesterday had left her weary, and she drifted into
sleep as she lay on the lounger. She did not hear Sam
and Pallas get up and go off to play tennis, and they,

considering her, decided it would be kinder to leave her.

She slept on for several hours, her skin beginning to redden as the sun poured down upon it, then woke with a stifled cry of pain as a hand touched her red shoulder.

Marc was crouching beside her, his face set grimly. "Now look at you!" he said furiously. "You have given yourself sunburn! I can't take my eyes off you for five seconds without you getting into some scrape or other!"

She turned and sat upright, wincing at the agony of her reddened back and shoulders. It felt as though red-hot needles were stinging along her skin. Her head swam dizzyingly. She looked at Marc, her eyes filling with tears.

"Oh, good God!" he groaned, and the next minute had picked her up into his arms and was carrying her, like a child, into the house.

CHAPTER SIX

THE doctor was back next day and tut-tutted over her, waving his small hands and talking rapidly in Greek to Pallas.

"He says you have been very silly," Pallas translated, smiling sympathetically.

Kate had had a bad night. She had tossed restlessly, her whole body apparently on fire. "I didn't realise the sun was so hot," she said wearily, on the point of tears again. She could not understand why she felt so emotionally disturbed. The slightest thing made her burst out crying.

The doctor bent over, shaking his head and spoke again.

Pallas translated again. "He says that the sun was unusually hot yesterday, but you should never go to sleep in the sun at any time. And he says," she paused, listening, "he says that the lotion should help, but the pain will be bad for another day or two. And you are to stay in bed and do absolutely nothing until he comes again. It is an illness which makes you depressed, like influenza, so try not to cry."

Kate looked up at the doctor and smiled faintly. "Thank him for me," she told Pallas.

The doctor nodded, as Pallas spoke and smiled back. Then he left, and Pallas tucked her up again, gently. "Would you like to sleep now, or shall I stay and talk?"

"I think I'll try to sleep," Kate said. "This lotion has made me more comfortable. I didn't sleep at all all last night."

"Poor Kate," sympathised Pallas. When she had gone Kate lay, in the semi-darkness of her room, gazing at the white shutters which Pallas had closed. Faint beams of light struggled through them and lay in bars across the floor. Her headache was better now, but her eyes felt hot and dry, and she was grateful for the cool shadows around her.

Marc had carried her up here yesterday and laid her gently on the bed. Through the hazy mist of pain she had stared up at him, wondering why he looked so savagely angry. She couldn't help getting sunburn. Then she had been suddenly, violently sick, and when she came back from her desperate race to the bathroom, she had found him gone, and Sophia waiting with cool water and gentle, soothing hands.

Her eyes closed. She preferred to forget what had happened yesterday. It had been a traumatic experience.

The next few days were quiet and peaceful. Pallas and Sam came in every morning. Sometimes they played cards with her, or just sat and talked. Sometimes she slept for most of the day. The burning sensation had lessened gradually. Her skin was now merely hot and dry. In places it was beginning to peel, and she watched it discontentedly. She was going to look a sight when it flaked off on her back. She would not be able to wear her bikini for the rest of the holiday.

On the Friday morning the doctor said she could

now get up. "But," he warned sternly, "no more sun-bathing. No exertion."

She promised eagerly. "It's been such a waste of a holiday," she said to Sam.

He was looking pleasantly tanned, his freckles merging with his healthy brown skin.

He gave her his hand. "Come on," he said, "I'll help you downstairs."

"I'm not an invalid," she protested.

Sam grinned at her. "You've been acting the part jolly well, then!"

To give herself confidence Kate had put on one of her new dresses, a cool white voile, very feminine and delicate, with a full skirt which reached half-way down her calf, soft frills which left her throat bare, and tight-fitting sleeves.

She met Mrs. Lillitos as she and Sam were going down, and the older woman smiled delightedly.

"My dear child, how enchanting you look! A vision from the past. But you need a hat." She smiled. "I have just the hat you need, *ma chère*." She walked stiffly back to her room, leaning on her cane, and returned in a short time with a large picture hat of white straw, trimmed with one very floppy pink rose.

Kate stood still while Mrs. Lillitos adjusted it. Sam watched, smiling.

"Great, kid," he enthused. "You look . . ." he hesitated, lost for words.

"Beautiful?" Mrs. Lillitos suggested teasingly.

Sam grinned. "You took the word out of my mouth, Mrs. Lillitos."

"And it covers up my sunburn," Kate told them

confidentially. "My back and arms are still very unsightly. I wanted to hide them."

They sat on the verandah, out of the treacherous sun, until lunchtime. There was no sign of Marc, and Kate did not dare to ask after him, but she gathered later that he had been engrossed in business during her illness, and had rarely emerged from his office, which was at the far side of the house.

They were about to move in for lunch when Marc came out on to the verandah. He stopped dead, catching sight of Kate, and stared at her in silence for a moment, then said politely, "You look much better. How do you feel?"

She murmured a vague reply. Sam and Pallas discreetly wandered into the house, leaving them alone. Kate stood up, feeling ridiculously overdressed. Marc was wearing a light blue shirt and casual grey slacks.

"I went up to the temple and told your fiancé about your illness," he said abruptly.

"That was very kind of you," she said stiffly.

"He would have come down to see you, but he had to finish his survey, and as sunburn is hardly a dangerous illness. . . ."

"I see his point," she said, quickly breaking in. "Of course he wouldn't come until he had finished."

Marc's lip curled. "You don't mind?" he asked. "You lack the usual feminine vanity, then. Doesn't it worry you that he couldn't care less whether you are ill or not?"

"You don't understand Peter," she said hurriedly.

During her illness she had had plenty of time in which to think about herself, and she had come to a decision about Peter. She had made up her mind to ask him if he would release her from their engagement. But she had no intention of letting Marc Lillitos know that. She did not want to discuss the subject with him.

Marc was watching her, with narrowed eyes. "Do you understand Peter Hardy?" he asked her coolly. "Do you realise what a selfish, irresponsible, cold-blooded fish he really is?"

She flushed and walked past him without answering. She was still engaged to Peter. She would not be disloyal to him now.

That afternoon, the other visitors arrived, and Marc drove down to the airfield to meet them.

Pallas was sulky as she sat with her mother and Sam, waiting for the black car to return. Mrs. Lillitos kept a stern eye upon her and checked an attempt she made to escape with Sam to play tennis, while Kate sat back, watching, wondering why Pallas was in such a strange mood.

The visitors arrived, talking in French which sounded like machine guns rattling away, and Kate hoped that they spoke some English, or the rest of the holiday was going to become a nightmare.

Marc came in, ushering two women before him, smiling down at one with great charm and courtesy.

She looked round and gave a little cry, "Madam!"

Mrs. Lillitos held out her arms, and the other woman hugged her warmly. "*Ma belle* Hélène," murmured Mrs. Lillitos, smiling.

She was a tall, slender woman, with deep brown hair, brown eyes and a look of quiet sophistication. Her coat and dress were cut very plainly, but with exquisite taste, in a striking violet. They looked superb on her.

Mrs. Lillitos looked past her to the other woman, standing beside Marc, one hand clinging to his sleeve, smiling up at him from wide brown eyes fringed by very thick black lashes. Her eyes were too heavily made up, giving her the appearance of a panda, with her thick white skin and black hair. She wore a figure-hugging black suit, very demure and yet very sexy. There was no blouse beneath it and the deep v-lapels revealed the white curve of her breasts and her slim white throat.

She was whispering to Marc and he bent his head, seeming amused, his eyes flickering over her appraisingly.

"Marie-Louise, *ma chère*," said Mrs. Lillitos firmly, and the other woman turned and walked over to her, still holding Marc's arm.

Kate stared at her. Was this, then, the French model with whom Marc was in love? She could not understand why he felt uncertain of her. She seemed madly in love with him, if one judged by her practised arch looks, her smiles and her air of possession.

She was very attractive, Kate had to admit. The silky dark hair was sleek and straight, drawn back from her face in a chignon. Her mouth was painted glistening red, her chiselled cheeks almost classically perfect. Yet there was a falseness, a coldness about her which made Kate dislike her.

Mrs. Lillitos introduced Sam and Kate to them, and Marie-Louise stared at her with insolence.

"A schoolteacher?" she repeated, then laughed, looking at Marc. She turned her head aside and whispered to him. Kate caught the words, "How irritating for you to have to put up with them, *mon cher*."

Marc did not reply. A man had come up the steps into the house and stood, watching them all with a smile. He was tall, dark and about twenty-four, with curly hair, pleasant brown eyes and a relaxed air.

"Jean-Paul," said Marc, "come and meet my sister's friends."

Pallas sat like a frozen statue, staring at her feet. The newcomer glanced at her, then at her brother, his brown eyes enquiring.

Marc said Kate and Sam's names. "This is Jean-Paul Filbert," he told them, "a cousin of ours."

He smiled at them, but his eyes rested longest on Sam, with curiosity and intentness. Sam was rather red, Kate saw. She wondered, suddenly, if this could be the man Pallas had told her about—the man Marc intended her to marry when she left college. Surely not? she thought. He's much older than Pallas. But she knew that, even these days, arranged marriages were common enough in Greece. And families always liked to keep their money in safe hands.

"Marc darling," drawled Marie-Louise, "give me a cigarette. I've run out."

He brought out his cigarette case and held it out to her. She took one and put it into her bright red mouth. Marc flicked open his cigarette lighter and held it to her cigarette, bending down. She took his hand in hers and held it steady, gazing up at him with provocative eyes.

"Thanks, angel," she murmured, leaning back.

Marc straightened. "Now you must excuse me. I am expecting a phone call from New York."

"Angel, you'll kill yourself," complained Marie-Louise. "Work and no play, you know. You don't want to be a dull boy, do you?" Her lashes flickered teasingly. "Why don't you relax and enjoy life?"

"I cannot afford to," he said, lifting his shoulders in a shrug. "Money, like children, needs constant attention."

"But so do I, my darling," she said, opening her eyes wide. "I am going to compete like mad, Marc. Business must be prepared for a battle."

"With me as the prize?" he asked lightly, grinning.

"Of course!" she said softly, "and a very valuable one. I will not share your attention with anything, especially not a telephone!"

Marc laughed. As he walked towards the door he passed Kate. Their eyes met. Hers were deliberately blank. He gave her a mocking, derisive flicker of a smile.

She understood what he meant without needing it put into words. That is how a feminine woman behaves, he was telling her. That is how a man wants his woman—flirtatious, flattering, attentive.

Mrs. Lillitos rose soon after Marc had gone, and said that she was going to her room to rest.

"I will come with you, Maman," said Hélène, slipping an arm around her. "We have so much to talk about, you and I."

Marie-Louise yawned. "I might as well have a nap myself. If Marc is going to be boring, I might as well not have come."

Sam and Pallas stood up, too, as Mrs. Lillitos walked slowly out of the room. Pallas said, "A game of tennis, Sam?" and Sam nodded.

Kate was taken back to find herself thus left alone with Jean-Paul.

"You are also going to sleep?" he asked her, as she rose instinctively.

She shook her head, smiling. "I think I'll take a stroll in the garden. I've been ill for a few days and I need the fresh air."

"May I come, too?" he asked, head to one side, scrutinising her.

"Why not?" she returned politely, and they went out into the garden.

They walked beneath an arched trellis, hanging with vines, out on to the lawn. The cypress trees and flower beds gave a quiet grace to the little garden, which was framed in a close-set hedge.

"Tell me about yourself," said Jean-Paul. "A schoolteacher, Marc said—how did you come to meet him?"

"I teach Pallas," she explained. "I teach music at her school, Cheddall."

He shot her a sidelong look. "Ah, yes, Pallas. And do you get on with her?"

"Very well," Kate said. "That's why I am here."

"And ... the young man? He is your brother? Is that why he is here? Because of Pallas?"

"They're friends," she said carefully.

Jean-Paul lit a cigarette, after offering them to her. For a while he smoked in silence. Then he said, "Pallas thinks herself in love with him, perhaps?" His tone was diffident, almost embarrassed.

She shrugged. "I really couldn't say. I don't have her confidence in this matter."

He looked sharply at her. Kate met his gaze directly and frankly.

He sighed. "I see. But perhaps you have your brother's?"

"No," said Kate firmly, "I've never discussed her with Sam. After all, it's a very private subject."

He laughed incredulously. "Love is never private, Miss Caulfield. It is, above all else, a family matter. That is why, as soon as I knew I loved Pallas, I spoke to her brother upon the subject."

She came to a halt and stared at him, with total disbelief. "You love Pallas? But she's only sixteen; years younger than you. Almost a child, still."

"She will be seventeen in two months," he said. "My mother was married when she was sixteen. I was born when she was seventeen."

"You are Marie-Louise's brother, though, aren't you?" she asked, puzzled. She had been sure Marie-Louise was older than him.

"I am her half-brother," he said. "My mother was Greek, a Lillitos. Her mother was French. Marie-Louise is five years older than me."

"Oh." Kate considered the information for a moment, then went back to Pallas. "Does Pallas know you love her?"

"She knows I wish to marry her," he said quietly. "I have not, of course, approached her alone. It would not be fitting."

Kate almost reeled with hilarious incredulity. "I can't believe it!" she exclaimed. "You talk like a Victorian novel!"

He flushed. "You are laughing at me," he said.

"I'm sorry, but I can't help it. No wonder Pallas was so awkward when you arrived!"

He was silent for a moment. Then he said, "You think she does not like me? Finds me unattractive?"

She looked at him, embarrassed, and saw the hurt look in his brown eyes. "Look," she said frankly, "Pallas is a modern girl. She doesn't want to be married off like a prize cow. She wants to . . ." she gestured vaguely, "live her own life."

"And I am not part of the life she wants?" he asked quietly.

"How do I know? How does she know, when she's never given the chance to choose freely? Perhaps you may be the man for her. But if you marry her against her will you'll never know if you are."

"I see," he said slowly. "You think I should back out now? Tell Marc I have changed my mind?"

"I shouldn't really advise you," she said. "You may think me prejudiced on my brother's behalf. To be honest, I don't believe that he and Pallas are in love. I don't believe they will ever be in love. But I think that if Pallas feels under pressure from you and Marc, she may convince herself she does love Sam, and that will be a disaster for everybody, including my brother, because I think Sam is the wrong man for Pallas. They're good friends, but they are too far apart for anything more intimate."

"O wise young judge," he said gently, taking her hand between both his and kissing it. "Thank you. I will speak to Marc tonight."

"And make sure he passes the word to Pallas," she said. "Insist on that being done immediately. Marc is capable of playing it by ear, and that might push Pallas too far."

He nodded. "I will be firm with him. And I am grateful to you for your advice. Several things Marc had said to me in his letters had made me suspicious of some other intervention. I was not surprised to see a young man here."

"Marc didn't tell you?"

"He never mentioned Sam to me," he said. Then, by common consent, they dropped the subject, and walked round, talking of the weather, Kate's sunburn, the world situation and other very natural subjects.

Dinner that evening was a far more lively occasion. The two new arrivals, Hélène and Marie-Louise, talked to Marc throughout the meal, ignoring everybody else. Pallas and Sam ate silently, and Jean-Paul devoted himself to Kate.

Their frank discussion had left them on a comparatively intimate level of friendship. He had discovered a shared love of Bach, and discussed various recordings with her, with almost professional enthusiasm and knowledge.

Kate felt Marc's eyes upon them from time to time, probing, curious, watchful. He was flirting lazily with Marie-Louise most of the time, fencing easily with her when she tried to provoke a show of jealousy by referring to her many admirers in Paris.

Her boasts of her conquests made Kate wonder if Marc were wise in not marrying her quickly. She could not believe that Marie-Louise did not desire to marry him. Everything she said, every look, said that she was ready and eager to be his wife. But was Marc not content, perhaps, merely to own the lovely French girl? Did he want to be certain of her fidelity? Perhaps he took her boasts of conquests too seriously, not seeing them for what they were—a blatant attempt to make him declare himself jealously.

After dinner Marie-Louise put a sleepy record on the turntable and she and Marc danced in the lounge, her black head upon his shoulder, leaning close to him.

Jean-Paul leaned over and asked Kate to dance. She smiled and stood up, going into his arms. She caught the exchange of looks between Pallas and Sam, her brother's raised eyebrows and grin. But Pallas was not looking as triumphant as she ought to do if she was really indifferent to Jean-Paul. She was, interestingly, frowning.

Jean-Paul looked down at Kate. "How am I doing?" he asked, with a mischievous grin.

"Is this part of your plan?" she asked, laughing. "To use me as a tease for Pallas?"

"You object?" he asked anxiously. "Your fiancé will mind, perhaps?"

"No," she said quickly, smiling, "he won't mind. And neither do I. It's in a good cause."

Jean-Paul looked relieved, and pulled her closer, bending his head to whisper in her ear, "You are a most unusual girl, Kate."

She smiled, then met Marc's glance over Jean-Paul's shoulder. Marc was not smiling. He was looking savagely angry again, the arrogant features dark and saturnine, the grey eyes biting.

Kate looked away. He was angry with her, of course, for flirting with his sister's promised husband. He probably thought her contemptible for attempting to steal Pallas's lover. She felt chilled, but tilted her chin defiantly. Let him think what he liked. She and Jean-Paul were going to set Pallas free to choose for herself.

Later, Jean-Paul spoke discreetly to Marc, who looked a little surprised, but gestured politely towards the part of the house in which his office lay. They walked out, in quiet conversation. Jean-Paul returned alone. He spoke softly to Kate, his face grave. "I have done it. I told Marc I had changed my mind."

"What did he say?" she asked involuntarily.

He shrugged. "He said very little—I was rather surprised. But he seemed displeased. Of course, there had been no official announcement. It was just an understanding between us, so there can be no gossip."

"Did he ask you why?" she queried, wondering what Marc had thought of Jean-Paul's unexpected change of heart. She could imagine him being very angry, particularly after the savage way he had looked at her while she was dancing with Jean-Paul.

"No, he seemed very thoughtful. Perhaps he has some business worry on his mind. Marc and I are old friends, but I felt a certain . . . how shall I put it? . . . distance, between us. I did not explain my motives to him, since I know he would try to persuade me to change my mind." Jean-Paul grinned at her. "He is an autocrat, as you must have realised. The Lillitos family obey him without question. And his business interests are so vast . . ." he lifted his shoulders in a Gallic gesture, "it is not surprising he is so dictatorial at times."

"It is irritating, though," she said, "and I don't

think one should pander to his god complex. He isn't a tinpot little divinity, whatever he thinks."

Jean-Paul looked both astounded and deeply amused. "A tinpot little divinity? Is that how you see him?" He stared into her blue eyes, smiling. "As I said before, you are a most unusual girl."

Next morning the sky was a little overcast and Kate decided to take the opportunity of sitting out on the beach again, while the sun was not so hot. Pallas and Sam walked down with her, carrying vast sun umbrellas, beach balls and towels, and they spread themselves out in luxury on the deserted sand of the little bay.

There was a pearly mist on the water, hiding the sun, but there was no wind, and Kate stretched out on a towel, gingerly lowering herself in case her back began to hurt again.

Her peeling skin was well coated with the doctor's soothing lotion. She slipped sunglasses on and lay with her face in the shade of a multi-hued umbrella, a plastic air cushion under her shoulders.

The sea murmured soothingly, flinging white-capped fingers upwards towards them, then falling back again in little ripples, leaving the sand ribbed and pale.

Pallas was reading the life of Beethoven, Sam was playing chess with himself and occasionally commenting rudely on his own weak moves. Kate did nothing at all, feeling her whole body limp and relaxed in the soft air.

She felt Pallas stiffening beside her, and looked up to see Jean-Paul and Marc coming down the beach.

"You look very comfortable there," Jean-Paul told

Kate, lowering himself beside her, "but should you be out here in the sun so soon?"

She peered up at the sky. "The sun is still hidden in cloud," she pointed out. "I have to venture forth sometimes, you know. I can't live in a tunnel like a mole."

He laughed and picked up her lotion. "Let me rub some of this into your arms before the sun comes out, then."

She had already done so, but she meekly allowed him to do as he pleased.

"Your skin is so fair," he murmured, his hand slowly stroking up to her shoulder. "It is like peaches and cream—I always thought that a silly expression, but now I know what it means."

Pallas leapt impatiently to her feet, sending up a shower of sand. "Sam, come and play beach ball!"

Obediently, Sam closed his pocket chess game and followed her down the beach.

Marc was leaning on one elbow, watching Kate and Jean-Paul like a cat at a mouse-hole, his grey eyes narrowed. She found his unmoving, unreadable gaze disconcerting. What was he thinking?

Pallas and Sam were running closer to them, shouting as they threw the ball from one to the other. Suddenly the ball landed with a thud on Jean-Paul's back, sending him sprawling over Kate. He landed, a hand on either side of her, almost knocking the breath out of her body, and they both began to laugh, after the initial shock.

"I'm so sorry," Jean-Paul apologised. "I hope I did not hurt you."

"Not at all," she smiled.

He withdrew slowly, looking down at her with a crooked smile. Over his shoulder Kate saw Pallas's sullen face as she took back the ball. Jean-Paul was about to lie down again when Sam said cheerfully, "Care to join us, Jean-Paul? Beach ball is more fun with three."

Pallas turned away, her dark hair swinging as she tossed her head, as though to emphasise her indifference as to whether Jean-Paul played or not.

He hesitated, his face uncertain. Kate smiled at him, "Yes, do play—I mustn't because of my back. I think I'll go to sleep for a while."

He stood up and slowly joined the other two. Pallas flung the ball at him, very hard, and it hit him in the stomach. Kate knew that Pallas had done it deliberately and felt like shaking the girl. But Jean-Paul straightened, looking steadily at her, and threw the ball back without a word.

Kate pulled her straw hat over her face and let her body relax. The sound of the sea, the balmy air, made her drowsy. Vaguely she heard the high voices of the ball players drifting away. The sea murmured on, gulls cried overhead and the sun came out mildly, caressing her skin. Behind her closed lids a warm orange flood of light seemed to focus, spreading through her like wine. She was lazy and content. Even the silent presence of Marc seemed distant.

Then she heard a movement beside her. Sand scattered over her bare legs. She opened her eyes and saw Marc, lying on one elbow still, but casually ladling handfuls of sand over her, like a child.

"What are you doing?" she asked resentfully, lifting her leg so that the sand fell away.

"What are *you* doing?" he asked, with an odd emphasis.

"Trying to sleep," she snapped. Was it impossible to stand still in any relationship? she wondered. One always seemed to move either forward or back, certainly in a friendship with the opposite sex. With Marc she moved between hostility and attraction. Were the two interchangeable? Like two sides of one coin? Today, again, she did not like him.

"Last night," he said conversationally, "I had a rather startling discussion with Jean-Paul."

Kate closed her eyes, straightening her leg again. "Oh?" She tried to sound bored, even indifferent.

"He was unofficially betrothed to Pallas," Marc said softly, "but last night he told me he had changed his mind."

"Really?" Kate yawned, flapping her hand over her mouth in a lazy gesture, her body stretching pleasantly with the movement. "Well," she went on, "Pallas is rather young for a man like Jean-Paul, I suppose."

Marc moved like a spring uncoiling, a hand on each side of her, bending to whisper forcefully. "What do you know of a man like Jean-Paul—you only met him yesterday!"

She could not pretend to be sleepy now. She lay staring up at him with a suddenly dry mouth. He was very close to her, his dark face tense and menacing, the strong muscles in his brown shoulders rippling as he pressed his hands down on the sand. He looked very handsome, very dangerous, and more attractive than she could bear.

"What does any woman know of any man she meets?" she countered warily, grateful for the sun glasses which helped mask her expression. "I just made a snap judgement, I suppose."

"You walked in the garden with him for an hour," he said bitingly. "I saw you from my office window. He kissed your hands. Rather fast work on his part —he was never the wolf type. You must have given him a lot of encouragement."

He was furious because Jean-Paul had broken his engagement to Pallas, she thought. But why take it out on me? He's looking for a scapegoat, but I'm not a volunteer.

Aloud, she said, "He is a Frenchman, isn't he? They kiss hands to be polite."

"He hasn't been able to take his eyes off you since he arrived," Marc said tightly, his lips curling at the edges.

"Is that my fault?" she retorted. "What am I supposed to do? Hang out a sign saying don't look?"

"You put up one saying don't touch," he sneered.

"That was only for your benefit," she flung, suddenly too angry to care, and then realised, with a sinking heart, that she had gone too far, and made him blazingly angry.

His dark face tightened as though she had struck him. He glared down at her, eyes glittering like points of steel, and his mouth swooped, closing on hers savagely, his hands gripping her sore shoulders.

For a second her heart seemed to stop, then it thundered into life again, pounding in her ears. Her eyes seemed darkened and aching. Her fingers curled imploringly, held rigid at her sides, as she fought the impulse to reach up and touch him.

Whatever happened, she must not let him guess

what that cruel, punishing kiss had done to her. As he drew away, breathing hard, she kept her eyes and lips tightly closed. After a moment she heard him walking away, his feet crunching on the sand.

Tears began to trickle down her face. So now she knew—what she had always known since their first meeting. She loved him. But now she had been forced, by her body's treachery, to admit it to herself.

CHAPTER SEVEN

WHEN the others came back she pretended to be asleep, and let them wake her, so that her silence could be put down to the drowsiness of someone suddenly dragged back to a wakeful condition. She trailed after them, back to the villa, dreading the first meeting with Marc, but when they arrived they found Sophia busily supervising the laying of the table, and she told them that Marc had taken Marie-Louise to Epilison to visit Pyrakis.

Kate felt a pang of unbearable jealousy at the news. She knew that Marc had only been reacting angrily, when he kissed her, to what he believed to be her interference between Pallas and Jean-Paul. The furious glitter of his eyes had confirmed that. But she stupidly felt hurt that he should take Marie-Louise to see Pyrakis so soon after taking her there.

She went up to change for lunch and chose a plain green linen dress which somehow expressed her depressed mood.

After lunch she played cards with Hélène Lillitos, who was bored. She found the other woman quite pleasant, out of the company of Marie-Louise. Hélène seemed to make an effort to be polite to her. Kate had noticed that she always wore black or lavender, and wondered if she were still mourning for her husband. But Paul Lillitos had died several years ago, so perhaps it was just that Hélène knew that the sombre colours suited her.

Occasionally, Hélène's slight French accent was tinged with an American twang, which reminded Kate of her usual residence in the United States.

She asked Hélène where she lived when she was in America, and Hélène explained that she had two homes.

"An apartment in New York and a little place in the hills in California. New York used to be an exciting place, but it is becoming a nightmare. One hardly likes to go out after dark, and never goes out alone." She shuddered. "So many of my friends have been mugged—you know?—robbed in the street. It is incredible that such things happen in such a civilised city."

Kate asked her about California, and Hélène went on to describe her other home. "In the spring and autumn it is beautiful, but it is too hot in summer."

"The Americans call autumn the fall, don't they?" Kate asked.

Hélène laughed. "Yes, the fall."

"It is such a descriptive word," said Kate. "It conjures up falling leaves, the dying summer, everything."

Hélène looked at her carefully. "You like words?" Then she smiled. "Of course, you are a schoolteacher."

Kate flushed at the slight condescension of the words. "I teach music, not English literature," she said, a little more sharply than she meant.

Hélène said quickly, "I am sorry, I did not mean to offend you."

Kate relaxed. "I shouldn't have snapped," she apologised in her turn.

Marc and Marie-Louise returned just before dinner. Kate saw them walking up towards the villa, holding hands and talking with animation, and she had to fight down a wild impulse to run away.

She was sitting beside Sam on the verandah, drinking an aperitif, and wearing her white voile dress. The weather had been rather sultry that afternoon. When the early morning mist lifted the sun was revealed, like a brass coin, in the sky, and as the day wore on the heat grew more and more oppressive.

Sophia darkly prophesied a thunderstorm that night, and Kate was inclined to agree with her. The lowering sky, the humidity, seemed to make one inevitable. Something of the same atmosphere lay on her own spirits. She felt tense, restless, nervous.

Marie-Louise gave Sam and Kate a brief, indifferent glance as she walked past, but Marc nodded to them, his eyes sliding over Kate without meeting hers. He was looking rather serious, she noticed. She felt relief flood into her when the other two vanished inside. The first encounter had passed somehow, and now she need not dread having to speak to him.

At dinner Jean-Paul was unceasingly attentive, talking to her, watching her, smiling at her. She was grateful for the shield of his presence. Behind that shield she could build up her defences again. Marc must not be allowed to bulldoze them down again.

She and Jean-Paul each had a need of each other. she was under no illusions about his flattering attentions. He wanted to heal his pride, wounded by Pallas.

The rest of the table was more divided. Pallas

barely spoke at all. Sam was absorbed by his shish-kebabs and sweet, orange-flavoured gateau. Hélène seemed distrait and nervous, and Mrs. Lillitos was apparently quite lacking appetite. Marc spoke anxiously as she sent away her plate, barely touched, but she unsmilingly shook her head, obviously telling him that she was quite well.

Kate looked back at the time before the arrival of Marie-Louise and Hélène, and wished it was back. There had been more ease in the party then. They had been quite happy.

After dinner Marc retired to his office. His mother went to bed, with Hélène in attendance, and Kate soon followed, feeling very low in spirits.

She heard voices from Mrs. Lillitos's bedroom, and thought that it was charming to see such affection between Hélène and her mother-in-law, particularly since Paul Lillitos had died so long ago. Would Marie-Louise get such a warm welcome into the family? She felt somehow, that Mrs. Lillitos did not like the other woman. She was always polite to her, yet there was a coldness between them. Marie-Louise was always cloyingly eager to flatter Mrs. Lillitos. Perhaps the older woman found that distasteful. Certainly the quiet warmth between her and Hélène was based, Kate thought, upon respect for each other.

She washed, cleaned her teeth and got undressed, then sat, in her frilly white nightie, staring at herself in the mirror. She was thinner, she thought. There were new hollows in her cheeks, a blue shadow beneath her eyes. Of course, she had been ill. Her appetite had not yet recovered since her attack of sunburn. But that did not account for the little droop at the corners of her mouth, or for those tell-tale shadows in her eyes.

A soft knock on her door startled her. She slipped on her dressing-gown and went to open the door. Her heart leapt into her throat. She stared, blue eyes wide and frightened, at Marc.

He was wearing an elegant dark lounge suit, formal white shirt and dark tie. He looked more like a successful businessman than ever tonight.

"Yes?" she asked, holding her voice steady by an effort.

He looked at her dressing-gown, which she had not buttoned, and which showed the scanty white nylon nightie beneath.

"I'm sorry," he said, his voice deep, "I did not realise you had gone to bed."

She pulled the dressing-gown closer. "What did you want?"

"To apologise," he said abruptly. "May I come in for a second? We need not close the door, if you are nervous about the conventions." Without waiting for an answer, he walked past her into the room. Kate looked down the corridor, saw nobody, and followed him, leaving the door ajar.

He stood by her dressing-table, looking down, his fingers lightly touching the lids of cosmetic jars, perfume bottles, her hairbrush. She waited, a few feet away, looking at the back of his dark head.

Then he seemed to jerk himself together, turned and looked at her, his face unreadable.

"I am sorry about that incident on the beach," he said formally. "I lost my temper."

"You blame me for Jean-Paul," she said quietly.

"You're wrong. You should never have agreed to that arrangement, you know. It's that that has been at the bottom of the trouble with Pallas all the time —she felt she was under pressure, being forced to marry him."

"Arranged marriages work very well," he said defensively, "and I am certain Pallas liked Jean-Paul very much. I should never have sent her to school in England. It has given her crazy ideas."

She flushed. "Like falling in love and choosing whom one marries?"

"Exactly so," he retorted. "You chose whom you should marry, and see what a mess you have made of your life!"

"You have no right to say that!" she said angrily.

"Isn't it true?" he asked thickly. "Can you deny that Peter Hardy is selfish and indifferent to you? All he thinks of is his work. He doesn't love you. He probably never has—or only for a short while. I do not suppose he will ever fall in love with anyone. He is too self-obsessed."

"You mustn't say this to me," she said weakly, unable to deny what had become obvious to her with every day that passed since their first meeting. No man who loved her could have abandoned her in a house where she would be thrown into Marc's company. Peter had not even noticed that she was uneasy with Marc. If he had loved her, he would have been aware of it.

"Your mother should have said it long ago," Marc said coolly. "Even Sam is aware of it. It is obvious to everyone but you. Peter does not love you, Kate, and I do not believe you love him."

She felt her cheeks flame into scarlet and her eyes seemed to lose the ability to focus. When her breathing settled a little, she said huskily, "My feelings are my own business. Was that all you wanted to say?" She was suddenly terrified that he might guess her feelings for him. He must go, she thought desperately. He must leave her alone before she betrayed herself.

Marc thrust his hands into the pockets of his elegant suit. "You won't listen to common sense, then? You hand out free advice to Pallas, to Sam, to me—why won't you take some back? Break off this ridiculous engagement and find someone you can really love and who is a man, not a dedicated boffin."

She was so afraid that he would read her love in her eyes that she said fiercely, "Perhaps I have—perhaps Jean-Paul is the answer to a maiden's prayer. Now, do you mind going? I'm sleepy."

Marc turned, like an automaton, his face rigid. "Very well, good night," he said stiffly, and then the door was shut and Kate was alone.

She rammed her fists into her mouth, quivering with agony. She could not possibly sleep now. She dressed again, in jeans and sweater, and slipped out for a stroll in the garden, but the thick heat of the air was no relief, and after ten minutes she went back indoors, where it was cooler.

As she passed Mrs. Lillitos's room the door opened and Marc came out, his shoulders unusually bowed. He straightened as they met, his eyes running over her jeans and sweater in surprise.

"You've been out?" he asked sharply. "Alone?"

"I was too hot to sleep," she said uncomfortably. He moved closer and looked down at her, the grey eyes narrowed. "Have you been thinking about what I said?"

Before she could answer his mother called quickly from within her room, and he turned back to answer her.

"Is that Kate?"

Kate looked in at the open door. "Yes, Mrs. Lillitos. I couldn't sleep as it was so hot."

Mrs. Lillitos was sitting in a deep armchair with a jigsaw puzzle on a tray in her lap.

She smiled. "Come and do this with me, then, my dear. I cannot sleep, either. I am afraid there is going to be a storm tonight, and I do hate them so."

Kate went into the room. "I'm not very good at jigsaws," she said, "but I would like to talk to you for a while. I hate storms, too."

Marc had followed her in, and was standing watching them. His mother looked at him severely.

"Go to bed, my son. You look very tired. I shall be quite all right with Kate to keep me company. Young company makes me cheerful, and Kate is such a pretty child."

He nodded. "Very well, Mama. Good night." He hesitated, then added coolly, "Good night, Kate."

His mother picked up a piece of blue sky. "Now, where does this go, I wonder? All these blue pieces look the same shape."

Kate hunted for a moment or two, then at last managed to fit the piece into place.

"It's a hard puzzle," she said. "Do you do many of them, Mrs. Lillitos?

"It helps to pass the time. Marc is so absorbed in

the business, and Hélène is always in the States. Even my little Pallas is away at school."

Kate felt herself flushing. Did Mrs. Lillitos know about Jean-Paul's change of mind? Had Marc told her that he blamed Kate?

The older woman's fragile hand suddenly reached out and took hers.

"*Ma chère*," she murmured gently, "there is no need to look so tragic. You are worrying about Pallas, no? Comfort yourself. I have had a long talk with Jean-Paul today. He told me everything."

Kate looked up, eyes wide. "Oh!" she breathed, with relief. Then, "You haven't told Marc?"

"Of course not, as Jean-Paul asked me not to do so, but I think you are both wrong. My son is quite capable of understanding the matter, if it is explained to him carefully. Pallas is a girl of temperament. Like a wild bird, she flies hither and thither, struggling. She needs Jean-Paul's steadiness, his gravity, his French formality. He would be the perfect mate for her."

"But, madame—" began Kate, and the other woman smiled and shook her head, interrupting her.

"I know, I know—Pallas must think she has chosen him herself. I agree."

"You do?"

"Of course," Mrs. Lillitos smiled. "Pallas wants to be hunted, to be caught, but only with her consent. She does not want to be sold like a cabbage in the market place."

Kate sighed with relief. "Exactly what I think."

"But do you think it wise for Jean-Paul to flirt with you in order to provoke her into an interest in him?"

asked Mrs. Lillitos seriously. "People may misunderstand." She carefully fitted several pieces into her puzzle, without looking up, and added, "As Marc does."

Kate's fingers trembled as she tried to fit another piece into an odd-shaped hole. Mrs. Lillitos gently took the piece away from her.

"No, *ma chère*, not there. . . ."

Kate looked up and their eyes met. Mrs. Lillitos searched the wide blue eyes thoughtfully, then Kate looked down again. They went on doing the jigsaw puzzle in silence until a sudden crack of thunder heralded the awaited arrival of the storm.

Kate saw her hostess flinch. "What we need," she said cheerfully, "is some soft music, to drown the sound of the storm. Have you got a radio?"

"We would waken the others," Mrs. Lillitos said regretfully. "But there is a record player in Marc's office. We could go down there, couldn't we? And his office is so far away from the bedrooms that we would disturb nobody."

"Won't he mind?" Kate asked anxiously. She did not want to run the risk of another row with Marc tonight.

"Why should he?" asked his mother, raising one fine eyebrow. She groped for her stick. "Give me your arm, *ma chère*, and we will solace our souls with music."

Kate laughed, and guided her down the stairs and along the corridor which led to Marc's office. She had never been in there before and for a moment her curiosity mastered her manners. She stared round her, taking in the long, red-leather topped desk, the steel filing cabinets, the bookshelves and cupboards. It was a long, wide room, probably the biggest in the house. The windows were covered with wooden shutters. There was discreet strip lighting down the middle of the room, and a thick grey carpet on the floor. Leather-backed chairs stood about the room. Everything was very tidy, very businesslike.

Mrs. Lillitos was watching her, with a faint smile. "You are interested in the room?"

Kate flushed. "I'm sorry, I was being curious."

"Naturally. *Ma chère*, my son works very hard. He is at the head of a vast modern business complex. It is not a... what do you say? A nine-to-five job. He works all the hours of the day, sometimes. He gets very tired, very irritable. Because, of course, he is only a man. And men have needs they are sometimes too proud to reveal."

Kate plunged across the room, desperate to change the subject, afraid of what she might hear. "Is this the record player?" She knew that she was behaving rudely, but she had to protect herself at that moment, against the pain of hearing his mother telling her about his need of Marie-Louise.

Mrs. Lillitos did not attempt to reopen the subject. She sat down in one of the thick leather chairs, and listened to the record Kate chose—a crashing piece of Wagner which rode down the storm and made it seem irrelevant.

When the music ended, the storm seemed to be blowing itself out, although rain still rattled against the shutters and the wind blew the cypresses until their branches scraped along the walls.

Kate put on another record, since Mrs. Lillitos

seemed reluctant to go to bed. This one was quieter, more conducive to a state of drowsiness.

"Ah, Bach," Mrs. Lillitos sighed, smiling. "Jean-Paul told me of your fondness for him. Marc, too, loves Bach, especially the Brandenburgs."

Kate forced herself to smile. She wished she had not been told that Marc loved her favourite composer. She wanted to be able to listen to Bach in future without being reminded of her brief, unhappy stay here on Kianthos.

They heard the record to the end and then went up to bed. Mrs. Lillitos smiled and touched Kate's hand, as they said goodnight at her door.

"You have been very kind to me, *petite*. I have never enjoyed a thunderstorm before!"

Kate laughed. "I'm glad you enjoyed this one—I did, too."

They turned to part, when a loud hammering startled them. It went on, growing in volume, and Marc's door burst open and he plunged out, wearing dark red pyjamas, his black hair on end.

"What is it?" asked his mother.

He shot her a look. "Someone on the verandah...." He vanished downstairs, and they more slowly followed.

"Who can it be at this hour?" Mrs. Lillitos wondered.

Behind them doors opened, but, as the banging had now stopped, after a moment, the doors closed again.

They found Marc standing in the hall with a young man wearing a soaking wet jacket. As they arrived he ran out again into the rain, and Marc came towards them, frowning.

"There's been a serious rock fall on the Etrusci road," he said grimly. "Alex is going to try to get across to Epilison by boat—the telephone lines are all down here." He turned towards the stairs. "I'll get over to Etrusci now," he said. "The worst of the fall crashed on the roofs of the side street. There are a number of people injured, Alex doesn't know how badly. They are just digging them out."

"I'll come with you," Kate said urgently, as he turned to go.

He stopped and looked at her, expression inscrutable. "You?" His mouth twisted oddly. "No, stay here. It will not be a very pleasant sight."

"I did a first aid course last year," she said quickly. "I learnt how to cope with civil disasters. I can bandage, diagnose . . . do all sorts of things."

He grimaced, hesitating. Over her head he looked at his mother. Then he said, "Oh, very well!"

Kate ran upstairs and got out her jacket, put on a pair of wellingtons which Marc threw at her as she passed his door, and which were rather big, then joined him as he came out of his room, in sweater and slacks, a thick waterproof in his hand.

He looked at her, one brow arched. "Where is your raincoat?" And when she explained that she did not have one, he went off and came back with one of his mother's. He pushed her into it as if she were a child, buttoning it quickly. Then he waved her down the stairs and followed.

Mrs. Lillitos hugged them both. "Be careful, my dears," she said, and shut the front door behind them.

They took the jeep and drove through the blinding rain at a speed which terrified Kate. She said nothing, but sat, twisted into a corkscrew of fear, beside him, grinding her teeth and clenching her fists on the side of the door.

They stopped, suddenly, as the jeep ran over something in the road.

"We are as far as we can go," Marc said, peering through the darkness and the sheeting rain. Kate could see practically nothing, but she followed him out of the jeep, carrying one of the boxes he had brought down with him.

They stumbled over rocks for a while, then came to a place where the road was completely blocked, and they had to climb down from the road, on slippery, muddy grass, Kate clinging to Marc's firm hand to guide her.

The village of Etrusci lay at the base of a sheer cliff. The storm had dislodged rocks from above, sending them crashing down on the end of the village. Fortunately, only some dozen houses were involved, but the people who had been in them were only now being dug out of the ruins of their homes.

When Kate and Marc arrived they found the local priest directing operations, his long black beard wagging furiously as he kept the men working. He turned aside to greet them, staring curiously at Kate, then smiling when Marc said something in Greek to him.

"I've told him you know some nursing," he told her. "He says the injured are being taken to his house. I'll take you there."

The men were working like demons, shifting the rocks and fallen walls with every tool they could find, including their bare hands. The rain poured down on them as they worked, soaking through their clothes and running down their faces.

The priest's house was already full of crying women, white-faced terrified children and shocked old men who sat rocking themselves like babies in corners.

Kate took off her raincoat, rolled up her sleeves and set to work. Marc left one of the first aid boxes with her, took the other and shot off to the site of the disaster again.

There were already two women working with the injured, a small middle-aged woman with a tight mouth and snapping black eyes, who seemed very efficient, but whose curt manner distressed the children even more than they were already distressed. And a plump, slow woman with a sweet smile who moved very lazily around the crowded room. They looked at Kate, spoke in Greek, and then went on working when she answered in English, shrugging.

Kate began to wash and bandage the arm of one weeping woman. She comforted her, wishing she knew some Greek, then moved on to a child who lay, with a blood-soaked dress, nearby. She found that the blood had apparently come from somewhere else, since the child was not hurt at all, only shocked into a state of complete dull disbelief. Kate stripped off the blood-soaked dress, washed the child gently and wrapped her up warmly in a blanket before giving her a small glass of pure glucose and water. The little girl coughed, made a disgusted face, but seemed less stupefied as the glucose took effect. Kate patted her cheek, smiled and went on to an old man who needed help.

She worked for what seemed like hours until she found that Marc was at her side, taking her arm.

"The doctor is here, with the Sisters from the convent at Epilison. They will cope from now on—come home, Kate. You look worn out."

She straightened wearily, pushing back a damp lank of hair from her perspiring forehead. Her back ached, her head was throbbing. Without a word she let him guide her out of the crowded house.

The doctor turned and smiled at her, shaking his head, and speaking severely, but with a great warmth and kindness in his black eyes. The two nuns with him nodded, like smiling children, their pale smooth faces approving.

Marc slid his arm around Kate, as she swayed a little. "The doctor says you are a silly girl, but very brave and very kind. You have done sterling work tonight, but now you must rest."

She managed to return the doctor's smile, then Marc had lead her out of the house, and the cool freshness of the night hit her like wine, making her head swim.

"Hey," Marc caught her, as she stumbled drunkenly, "you aren't going to faint, are you?"

She laughed, her voice sounding high and unstable even to herself. "I feel quite drunk!" she confessed, giggling. "Everything is going round, like a fair-ground."

Marc supported her gently. "Can you walk to the car? The road is still blocked."

"I think so," she said, trying to stop giggling. The road was awash with rain, but the purple sky was now clear and cloudless. To the east there were a few grey wisps of light, heralding the coming dawn, but the stars still flashed, far off, like tiny diamonds, and the moon sailed, like a slice of lemon, above the shadowy hills.

They picked their way carefully back over the rocks which littered the road. Marc helped her into the jeep, climbed in and began reversing slowly, sounding his horn, to warn anyone coming up the road behind them. At a convenient widening he managed to turn the jeep and they drove home fast.

Kate swayed with the movement of the jeep, her head feeling almost loose on her shoulders. So much had happened tonight and she had worked with such intent concentration that she had lost sight of everything else but the job in hand. Now the loss of a night's sleep was catching up with her. Her eyes were raw and dry, as if rubbed with sand, and her throat hurt.

The greyness in the sky grew as they drove. "It will be morning soon," Marc murmured as they drew up outside the villa.

Kate climbed out and stretched, yawning. Through the trellised tunnel at the side of the house she could see the green lawns of the garden, glistening with rain, and on a wild impulse she ran round into the cypress-lined garden. She stood, breathing in deeply, enjoying the fresh night scents.

Marc came up behind her. "You English lunatic," he said softly, "come into the house. You have been up all night and you are asleep on your feet."

She laughed and turned back. "I wanted to feel . . ." she paused, not knowing quite how to describe the feeling she had been possessed by at that moment.

"Alive?" he suggested gently. "I understand. It was grim, wasn't it? Nature can be very cruel."

"Yes," she whispered, remembering the child in the bloodstained dress. She had found out later that the child had lost her father in the rock fall. His body had been found in the ruins of his house. Only the arrival of her weeping, white-faced mother had snapped the little girl out of her dangerous state of suspended grief, and they had clung together, loudly weeping, yet comforting each other.

Marc propelled her by the elbow into the villa. They went into the kitchen, which was large, beautifully equipped and tiled in orange and black.

Marc made Kate sit down while he put the kettle on the stove. "A cup of tea is what the English love most," he teased. "That will restore you!"

She sighed longingly. "It sounds heavenly! My mouth is as dry as a kiln."

He stood over her, very tall and dark. "Pyrakis said your mouth was cool and sweet and inviting," he reminded her softly.

Kate was too weary to respond. She shook her head, so that her blonde hair fell loose from the band that had held it in place all evening.

Marc knelt down beside her and took off her muddy wellingtons, flung them behind him carelessly, and took off her damp socks. He treated her, she thought, as if she were a small child. Then he brought her a bowl of warm water and some soap. "Wash your face—it will make you feel better," he said, "and then soak your feet. We don't want you catching a chill."

He stood with his back to her, making the tea with slow, deft movements. She carefully washed her hands and face, feeling relief as the sticky grime and perspiration were peeled off, leaving her skin cool and clean. Then she put the bowl on the floor and let her feet soak gratefully. They were sore and hot, and the water lapped round them deliciously.

She looked down at her clothes with a grimace. Her white sweater was filthy. Blood stains, mud, green streaks of grass, made it look as though she had been in a major disaster. The jeans were in no better condition. One leg was matted with dried blood and the bottoms of both were black with mud from the wet roads.

"I look a sight," she said, yawning.

Marc put a fragrant, steaming cup of tea in front of her. A slice of lemon floated on the top. She yearned foolishly for English tea, milky and sweet, but this was better than nothing. As she lifted the cup to her lips Marc muttered something, and she looked up, eyes enquiring.

"The veins are standing out on your wrist like whipcord," he said curtly.

Kate looked incuriously at her wrists. He was right. Beneath her pale skin blue veins stood out visibly. "They always do when one is tired," she pointed out. "I expect yours do, too."

He shrugged. "I am more used to late nights, perhaps. You must stay in bed all day tomorrow. We do not want you to be ill again. This has been an unfortunate holiday for you."

In more ways than one, she thought miserably. She drank her tea and stood up to reach the towel he had placed on the table for her. Marc walked to the side of her chair and took it from her grasp, crouched down and lifted one of her feet. She sat down again, suddenly, in case she fell over.

"I'll do that," she said quickly.

He took no notice of her. Gently, slowly, he wiped the foot dry, holding it on his knee. Then he put it down on the floor and took the other, and did the same.

Kate stood up quickly, her heart quickening. She suddenly could not bear to be here with him any longer. It was too agonising to have him being so kind in that impersonal fashion. She did not want him to treat her as a child. She was a woman.

"Good night, then," she said brightly, edging towards the door.

He smiled at her. "Sleep well. I'll tell Sophia not to wake you. You can stay in bed as long as you like."

She nodded and opened the door.

"Kate," he said suddenly, moving towards her. She halted, looking round uneasily at something in his voice which she could not quite identify.

"I haven't thanked you yet," he said quickly. "You worked like a Trojan tonight. I am very grateful to you."

"It was nothing," she dismissed. "Anyone would have done it."

"Not quite," he shook his head. "Only someone kind and brave. You got filthy, you are very tired and you were very upset by some of the things you saw. Don't push my thanks away, Kate."

She flushed, then smiled. "I'm sorry, I didn't mean to be curt."

"You are tired," he nodded. "Go to bed, my . . . my dear."

Kate looked up, smiling at him, and he slowly bent his head towards her. Her heart quickened into a thunder. She waited, lids drooping, lips slightly parted.

Then a voice behind them said sharply, "Marc, what is going on here?"

Marc straightened, stiffening, and his eyes went over Kate's head to the woman standing behind her, in the open doorway.

Marie-Louise repeated her question, in a high, shrill tone. "Why are you here, in the middle of the night, dressed like that? Where have you been?"

Kate turned blindly and pushed past her without a word. As she fled up the stairs she heard Marie-Louise say, "You haven't been making love to the little schoolteacher, have you, darling? You really must not flirt with people like that—they don't understand your little games! They take them seriously and get hurt."

CHAPTER EIGHT

SHE slept all the next day, dreaming constantly of Marc. She seemed to be fighting her way towards him, through thick jungle, constantly aware of snakes underfoot which uncurled and slid away from her, hissing, making terror flare inside her. She kept catching sight of him, tall, dark and elegant in formal clothes, with a woman on his arm. Jealousy and despair made her fall back, sobbing, but then she would hurry onwards. Always he was just out of her reach.

Then, just before she woke up, she finally caught up with him, and he turned and looked at her with cold, indifferent eyes. She gave a cry of pain—and woke up, the cry still on her lips, to find herself in the darkened bedroom.

She sat up and looked at the tiny jade clock which stood on her bedside table. It was four o'clock, she saw. She swung her legs out of the bed and went to the window. The shutters swung back, letting the sunshine stream into the room. The light made her blink and her head throbbed. She sat down on the end of the bed, stretching sleepily.

There was a knock on the door a moment later. Kate called, "Come in," expecting Sophia, but it was Mrs. Lillitos who entered, smiling at her as she slowly limped across the room.

"I was in my room when I heard your shutters

open," she said. "I have rung down for your breakfast, my dear."

Kate laughed. "Breakfast? I'm afraid I've slept later than I intended. I'm so sorry."

"Nonsense. You had every right to sleep after being up all night. I slept very late myself. I thought we might eat together in here."

Kate smiled, "That would be very pleasant."

Sophia came in shortly afterwards, with a large tray, and smiled warmly at Kate.

"*Kalimera, kyria!*"

Kate had begun to learn a little Greek from Sophia since her arrival, and was able to answer. "*Kalimera, Sophia!*"

Mrs. Lillitos laughed. "Ah, you are learning Greek. That is very good."

"I only know a few phrases which Sophia has taught me—good morning, good night and so on . . ."

"One must make a start somewhere," said Mrs. Lillitos, looking oddly delighted.

Sophia laid the tray down on the long table under the window. She whipped off the cloth which covered it, revealing orange juice, toast, coffee and boiled eggs. A pot of English marmalade made Kate laugh.

"It looks delicious, Sophia. *Efharisto!*"

"Thank *you*," Sophia emphasised, smiling, and went out.

"We are all grateful to you for what you did last night," Mrs. Lillitos explained. "Sophia has a nephew who lives in Etrusci. You comforted his wife while she waited to hear if he had survived."

Kate thought back to the horror of the night before. "The tiny, dark girl who was very pregnant?

Oh, I wish I had known she was related to Sophia. I might have said something more comforting. I felt so helpless, not being able to speak the language. But her husband was safe, so all ended well."

Mrs. Lillitos smiled. "I think she understood your feelings, even if she did not know what you were saying. You have such very expressive eyes, Kate. They are the mirror to your heart."

Kate flushed hotly. Were they? she wondered uneasily. And if so, had Marc read their message last night, and seen her helpless love for him? Humiliation and shame burnt in her chest. She made herself eat her breakfast, although it almost choked her.

Marc tapped on the door as they finished. He was looking alive and vital this morning, his blue sweater and casual dark blue slacks very neat compared with the clothes he had worn last night. He grinned at Kate. "How are you? You look very pretty."

She became hotly aware of the scantiness of her nightdress and looked around for her dressing-gown.

"Come back, later, my son," his mother said sternly. "Kate is *en déshabille*, and not ready to receive male visitors."

"I only came to tell her that her fiancé has arrived. I sent for him this morning." His grey eyes danced challengingly. "I thought she might want to see him."

Kate felt her nerves jump, but she kept her face under control. "Thank you," she managed to say stiffly.

His mother went slowly to the door. "Come down when you are ready, my dear," she said gently. "There is no hurry."

The door closed and Kate was alone. Now there

could be no doubt left in her mind about Marc's feelings towards her. If he had cared about her at all would he have sent for Peter? Was this his way of telling her that he was not interested in her and that she should concentrate on her fiancé?

Of course, he did not know, and she would never tell him, that she had decided to break her engagement.

She had faced this decision days ago. It had been a mistake to become engaged to Peter. It was fortunate that she had realised it in time. It would have been a disaster if she had married him and only then discovered their total indifference to each other. Marc had been so right when he said that Peter did not love her, nor she Peter. But, believing that, why had he brought Peter here now?

A flash of intuition came to her and she bit her lip. Of course! He was trying to protect his sister. He thought that she was interested in Jean-Paul and he had brought Peter here in order to put a stop to all that.

Dully, she dressed in her plain green linen dress and went downstairs. She found the lounge empty. Sophia bustled past and stopped to tell her that Peter was in Marc's office and the others all down at the beach.

The storm had again left the weather golden and sunny. Kate stood on the verandah staring up at the bright blue sky. It seemed cruel that the world should be in such a holiday mood when she was so miserable and depressed. It ought to be raining all day.

Then she laughed at herself. What a conceited, self-obsessed thought! As if she was the only person in the world!

Peter erupted on to the verandah beside her, his fair hair wildly standing on end, his eyes furious.

"Kate," he began hotly, "you must go and talk some sense into Lillitos!"

She looked at him in startled amazement. "What?"

"He says there's to be no expedition," Peter shouted. "He just said he's changed his mind. He won't allow anyone else to dig up there. He doesn't want strangers on the island. The man's insane. It mustn't be allowed!"

Kate looked at him silently for a moment. He had not seen her for over a week, she thought with wry resignation, and in that time she had been very ill with sunburn, been involved in a disaster, and for all he knew, was still weary. Yet he did not even greet her. No kiss, no word of pleasure in seeing her again. All that interested him was the temple up there on To Angkistri.

"I can't interfere," she said quietly, at last. "You must cope with it on your own, Peter."

He glared at her. "Kate, this is vitally important. The temple is the most wonderful thing that's ever happened to me in my life. It shows clear signs of a number of periods, so it's been in continuous occupation for generations. It was first founded in Mycenean times, but the pillars and roof were obviously much later. Oh, Kate, for God's sake—can't you see what it means?"

"Peter, I want to ask you a question," she said clearly.

He shut his mouth on what he had been about to say. Impatiently he waited, fidgeting.

"Do you love me?"

He gave her an incredulous look, running his fingers through his hair. "What? My God, Kate, don't drag in irrelevancies at this time! I have too many important things to think about!"

"Aren't I important, then?" she asked.

He looked embarrassed. "Oh, I'm very fond of you, of course, you know that! We're engaged, aren't we? What's the point of these questions, Kate?"

"Never mind your damned temple," she snapped, suddenly angry. "Listen to me for a moment. You don't love me, Peter. You are, as you said, mildly fond of me, but if I vanished tomorrow, I doubt if you would even notice."

"Oh, really," he said crossly, "how like a woman to try to put everything on a personal level! Can't you think of anything but yourself? This is a crisis in my life. I need your help, and you're trying to make me pay for it with declarations of undying passion, I suppose."

Kate was so angry she could hardly speak for a moment. "I'm doing nothing of the kind! I only want a little honesty between us. I'm trying to be honest with you."

He looked at her, then, with more awareness. "Oh, I get it! You want to break off our engagement? You've found someone else?"

"No!" she said roughly, "I haven't found anyone. I just . . . want to sort things out honestly."

"You do want to end things, though?" he asked.

She hesitated. "Oh, yes," she said on a quick breath. "Yes, I do. I don't love you. I'm fond of you, but I don't really love you."

He shrugged. "Well, now that's settled, can we talk about the temple?"

She glared at him. "You don't give a damn, do you, Peter?" She pulled off her ring and threw it at him. He caught it awkwardly, looked at it with amazement and stuffed it into his pocket. "The temple—" he began, but Kate had fled.

Peter stared after her, grimacing. "Women! Really!"

Marc came out on to the verandah, smiling gaily, and Peter grabbed at his arm.

"Look, Lillitos, about this expedition . . ."

Marc grinned at him, eyes dancing, "Try again next year," he said. "Perhaps I'll change my mind again. By the way, if you wish to leave right away, my plane is waiting on the airfield. I have had all your gear put aboard. When you have drawn up all your plans for the expedition, write to my office in Athens, to my personal secretary, Achille Danelos. He will get in touch with you and make the necessary arrangements. If there is an expedition, it must be a small one, and for the summer months. Right?"

Peter let out a long relieved sigh and grinned. "Thank you very much. I'm very grateful."

"Jake will drive you to the airfield," said Marc. "Off you go."

Peter looked a little startled. "Now? But I wanted to see Kate . . ."

"I think she has said all she wants to say," Marc said politely. "If you do not leave now it will soon be too dark. My plane will take you to Athens. I have booked a flight for you tomorrow at noon. You can pick up the ticket at the airport. It is in your name. Goodbye."

Stunned, Peter obediently walked towards where Jake was waiting with the car. Suddenly he stopped, holding out the little ring. "Will you give this to Kate for me?" he asked Marc.

Marc looked at it, lying sparkling on his palm, and his lip curled scornfully. "I do not think so," he said, with hauteur. "Keep it for your next fiancée."

Peter reddened, looked angry, then drew himself up and walked away. He did not dare to antagonise the man, he thought. The expedition depended on the whims of this rude, spoilt millionaire. And anyway, Kate was right. They had not been suited. She had never really been interested in his work. And if a man couldn't depend upon his wife to share his interests, what point in marrying? He looked forward to the excitement there would be in archaeological circles when he dropped his bombshell. And he broke into happy whistling, forgetting Kate and everything else.

Kate wandered for a long time around the cliffs, then turned back and found herself in .. myrtle grove. She stood, breathing in the fragrance of the cooling air. The heat of the sun was slackening and the moths had begun to flit over the thyme, their dusty wings glowing.

She thought back over the six years of her relationship with Peter. How had she come to think herself in love with him? She remembered how different he had seemed, when she was a young girl, with his blond beard and vague professor-like air. The boys she had known then had all been crazy, half-grown lads. Peter had seemed so mature. And from a girlish crush she had let herself drift into a long-term relationship with no solid base.

She knew now that she had never been in love with him. He had never made her heart stop, as Marc did. His kiss had never exalted and petrified her. She could not blame Peter. It had been her own fault for allowing herself to be fooled by such a vague response. He had been too amiable to hurt her, and she had never seriously thought about his feelings.

Well, they were both free now, to find real love. At least, Peter was—she was not free. She knew that she would never love anyone as she loved Marc.

She heard a twig crackle nearby and turned to see Jean-Paul, looking lost and fed up, wandering towards her.

He smiled politely. "How are you today, Kate? You look pale. Marc told us how brave and good you were last night. I admire your courage."

She shrugged his compliments away. "Thank you, but really, it was only a little thing. You're looking rather cross yourself."

He grimaced. "Pallas barely speaks to me. How can I woo her when she will not let me near her?"

"She jealous," Kate explained, "and uncertain of herself. After all, she isn't seventeen yet. Give her a chance. You're in too much of a hurry. Wait a while."

"Easy for you to say," he said forcefully, "but hard for me to follow your advice. Do you really think she is jealous?"

"I'm certain of it. She's been very offhand with me since you arrived."

Jean-Paul looked delighted. "Then you think she cares something for me, after all?"

"I'm almost sure she does. It might only be pique, of course. But time will show you the truth."

He took her hand, stopped and held it up to stare. "Your ring? You have lost your engagement ring!"

"I'm no longer engaged," she said, flushing.

He looked appalled. "*Ma chère*, I hope this is not my doing! I would not have done that for the world . . ."

"It has nothing to do with you. My fiancé did not even know of your existence. It was a mutual agreement. We just did not suit."

He looked a little embarrassed. "I see . . ."

She looked up at him and laughed. "Really, Jean-Paul, you are quite irrelevant, I assure you. I am not in the least attracted to you, which is what you are afraid of, I think?"

Very red, he met her teasing eyes. He laughed, a little shamefaced and embarrassed. "Pardon! I was nervous for a moment. The freedom of English girls astounds me. You are so . . . forthright!"

She grinned. "Well, it clears the air to know how you stand, doesn't it? Shall we go in to dinner?"

Dinner was, oddly, a very gay occasion at first. Marc was in volatile spirits, keeping up a barrage of teasing humour, his eyes constantly dancing.

But as the meal went on his mood seemed to deflate a little. Kate, who was quietly talking to Jean-Paul most of the time, was curiously aware that Marc's smile came less and less, and that he was more and more silent. She wondered if he were feeling the effect of his very late night. Had he slept at all since?

When she glanced furtively at him she saw shadows beneath his eyes and tension lines around his mouth which seemed to show that he had not.

Jean-Paul poured her another glass of retsina, his fingers touching hers as she held her glass towards him. He smiled at her gravely and she smiled back with warmth, liking him very much.

It was comforting to feel that she need not be stretched nervously, on edge against the probing intelligence Marc always aimed at her. With Jean-Paul she could relax, be herself, unselfconscious. He was a very quiet, steady young man, without Marc's vitality and tension.

She saw Pallas sullenly pushing her unfinished meal away, pouting, her small dark face all angles and frowns. What Pallas needed, she thought, was the sort of calm background Jean-Paul would give her.

"Shall we dance, *chérie*?" Marie-Louise asked Marc, as they drank their coffee in the lounge later. "Put some records on and let us dance!"

Marc shrugged, "Why not?"

He crossed to the cabinet and selected some records. As the music swirled out, sweet and soft, Marie-Louise archly turned out most of the wall lights around the room.

"Dancing in the dark is more romantic," she said to Marc, her thick lashes fluttering invitingly.

The room was shadowy now, the only lights left on being one at each end. Marc and Jean-Paul cleared a central space, moving the furniture back against the walls. Then Marc turned to Marie-Louise, with a brilliant smile, and she glided into his arms. Pallas looked up at Sam, her face urgent.

"Shall we dance, too?"

"What? This is music for the oldies," Sam said scornfully. "I don't know how to dance to it."

Kate laughed. "Just put your arms round Pallas and let your feet move in time to the music," she advised, and added teasingly, "I won't tell your friends when we get back home. Cross my heart!"

Sam grimaced at her. "I shall feel a fool!"

"I know how to dance to it," Pallas said shyly. "I learnt at my last school—the waltz, the polka and the military two-step."

"Good grief!" Sam shuddered. "Did they wear chastity belts, too? What a freaky establishment!"

Kate kicked his ankle. "Dance!" she commanded.

He grinned, shrugged, and got up, giving Pallas his hand with a grimace of resignation.

Jean-Paul had watched and listened in silence. Now he moved nearer Kate and said steadily, "And shall we dance now, Kate?"

She nodded and they moved off, dancing very formally. He danced, as he did other things, with precision and care. Neatly his feet slid from step to step. He revolved, reversed, guided her through the dance, a slight polite smile on his well cut lips, but not speaking.

Kate looked up at him. "You look as if you're hating every minute!" she said gently.

He looked down and the gravity of his expression melted a little. "You dance very well, *au contraire*," he murmured, smiling.

She stood on tiptoe and whispered in his ear, her face very close to his, "When you dance with Pallas tell her how pretty she looks tonight."

He looked puzzled. "I thought I was not to dance with her? I thought I was to . . . be indifferent?"

"Alter tactics now and then," she advised, still whispering. "See what a little change brings."

The record came to an end. Kate moved out of Jean-Paul's arms, nudging him discreetly. He turned to Pallas and asked her to dance with him next, and she flushed and glanced uneasily at Kate, who smiled cheerfully and took Sam's hand.

"Come on, brother, let me teach you how to do these oldie dances now!"

Marc interrupted her abruptly, leaving Marie-Louise and pushing Sam aside.

"No, no, we cannot have brother and sister dancing —Sam can learn the steps from Marie-Louise." He slid his arm round Kate's waist and she felt her heart squeezed inward, as though by a giant hand.

Marie-Louise looked hard at them, her eyes brilliant with fury. Sam stood awkwardly, trying to smile at her, but she pushed past him, flinging a careless, "I am going to get myself a drink . . ." as though he were a little boy.

Kate looked up at Marc. Didn't he realise how Marie-Louise resented his dancing with her? He was gazing past her, his jaw taut, the grey eyes hidden by drooping lids. She could not read his expression at all.

Anyway, she thought defiantly, why should she worry about Marie-Louise? Let Marc deal with her. She was here, in his arms, for a brief while, and she determined to enjoy it.

As though he read her thoughts he glanced down, the arrogant mouth relaxed. "We dance well together, don't we?" he said, very softly, his arm tightening round her waist.

She laughed, a little breathless with excitement, and a pink flower bloomed in each cheek.

His left hand gripped hers more firmly, his thumb sliding over the back of her hand and touching her ringless finger. "There is a white band where your ring was," he said teasingly. Over dinner he had mentioned, very casually, that Peter had already left the island.

Kate threw a glance up at him. "You know I've broken my engagement, then?" she asked unsteadily.

He grinned wickedly. "I heard every word," he admitted shamelessly. "I was eavesdropping."

She flushed hotly. "How could you?" she burst out. "You shouldn't have . . ." She remembered the conversation between herself and Peter. Marc had had no right to listen.

He pulled her nearer to him, bending his head to whisper to her, "You took my advice, though," he said with irritating self-assurance. "I knew you did not love that fellow."

Burning with humiliation, she tore herself away and ran out of the room, through the front door and out into the quiet garden. As she plunged beneath the cypresses she heard him following her and turned angrily to face him, chin tilted defiantly.

"Please leave me alone," she said, her voice wavering.

Marc stood, facing her, very tall and dominating, his hands in his pockets. Over the top of the hills the moon swam, like a silver crescent, trailing misty clouds. The wind stirred slightly in the branches of the trees. From the house she could hear the faint sounds of sweet music and a patina of yellow light streaked the darkness by the door.

"You don't mean that," Marc said, his accent sounding foreign for once, his voice thickened and uneven.

"I do!" she flung bitterly, hating him for that moment. She was so afraid that he had guessed her love for him that she could almost have killed him at that moment. Her pride fought bitterly against her love, poisoning it.

He stepped closer and looked down, eyes glittering in the moonlight. His profile was dangerously masculine, the light shafting on the narrow planes of his cheekbones and jaw. "If I thought for a moment that you did—" he began slowly.

"Go away!" she whispered frantically, her hands pushing at his chest.

But at her touch, as though a dam burst, he grabbed her shoulders and pulled her close against him. She trembled, feeling the hard litheness pressing against her. "No, Marc," she whispered in terrified appeal.

"I've had enough of being treated as an old-fashioned villain," he retorted harshly. "Like all women, you are not honest enough to admit your own motives. You make up fantasies and hide behind them. Well, I will not let you fashion a fantasy about me. I'm real." He bent her backwards, his hands cruelly hurting her shoulders. "Look at me, Kate!"

She nervously glanced upwards. His face was very close, the features etched sharply in the moonlight. His mouth had a cruel tightness below the mocking eyes. Then he slowly lowered his mouth until it touched hers. She gasped, trying to shrink away, and he pulled her nearer. His lips whispered, against hers, "You want this as much as I do—do you think I don't know that? You can't hide from me for ever, Kate. I want you. . . ."

Then his mouth was moving, hotly, urgently against hers, and she felt her body melting in passionate response. Through the rising passion and clamour of her pulses she dimly tried to reason with herself. He had not said he loved her. But her own desire was breaking loose from the bonds she had placed on it, and she knew she would not be able to resist much longer. She loved him too much.

The sudden interruption was like a douche of cold water on inflamed nerves. From behind them came a peal of silvery laughter, and Marc's arms dropped from Kate, his head jerking upwards, a blind look on his face.

Marie-Louise stood there, head to one side, an artificial smile of false amusement painted on her red mouth. "*Chéri*, I am so sorry to spoil your fun, but there is an urgent call for you from New York. They said it could not wait."

He muttered furiously beneath his breath, looked at Kate, hesitated, then walked quickly into the house.

Marie-Louise smiled at Kate, her eyes hard and glittering. "Marc is an exciting lover, *n'est-ce pas*? I hope you enjoyed your little interlude with him." She held up a hand, as Kate stirred in restless anger, "*Mais non*, I am not jealous, *ma petite*. There have been so many pretty little girls! Marc likes his girls blonde, sometimes, for a change, but he prefers brunettes. I would not want you to misunderstand him. He is a flirt, you understand? He likes to conquer. You saw in England—he collects scalps!"

Kate was aching with bitter misery, but she managed to hold up her head in cool scorn. "Why are you telling me all this?"

"To save you from being hurt. I know how serious you English girls can be—you might think he meant his little attentions. When I marry Marc all this will stop, of course, but until I am ready to give up my career I do not feel I can interfere with his pleasures. After all, he is a man! So please enjoy yourself with him as you wish, but remember—be prepared for dismissal when he is tired of you."

Kate's face was burning with humiliation now. She laughed, fiercely. "Thank you, Mademoiselle Filbert. You are too kind!"

"Ah, you are cross," said Marie-Louise sweetly. "I did not mean to hurt your feelings, or make you feel ashamed. Believe me!"

Kate walked away, with the mocking laughter ringing in her ears. She went to her room and sat on the bed, clutching her head in ner hands. Humiliation, pain, shame drove her wild. She bit her inner lip until it bled, then threw herself down on to the bed and gave herself up to a silent sobbing, her head buried in the pillow.

Echoes kept reaching her inner ears. So many pretty little girls, that woman had said. And: Marc is a flirt, you understand, he collects scalps. Well, she had suspected as much from the beginning. It was only confirmation of what she already knew. But how it hurt! She had revealed herself to him, left herself exposed to his mockery. Now he knew that he could have her if he wished—what next?

She must get away, she thought, her pride stung. But how? She was forced to wait until Marc allowed her to leave, and every moment she spent in his company was dangerous. She never wished to see him again.

So he thought he would amuse himself with her, did he? Play until Marie-Louise condescended to marry him? What had she said? Be prepared for dismissal when he tires of you? The insolence of it!

Then her blood ran hotly as she remembered the way he had whispered that he knew she wanted his kisses. She had noticed at the time that he had not mentioned love, only said that he "wanted" her. Well, now she knew what he had meant!

She had locked the door of her room. Suddenly she heard the door knob turning. Someone knocked. She sat up, rubbing her face.

"Who is it?" she whispered.

"Marc! Let me in!"

She stiffened. How dared he come here like this! Scarlet, hollow-eyed, she went to the door. "Go away!" she hissed. "Leave me alone!"

She heard him groan, "Oh, for God's sake, not again! I thought we had had that out!" And there was a note of tender amusement, of indulgence, in his voice which stung her.

"I meant it the first time," she said, "before you forced your disgusting attentions on me!"

There was a silence. "Kate," he said, his voice sharp now, "open this door!"

"I certainly will not!"

Again a pause, then he said, almost pleadingly, "Kate, I have to fl, to Athens tomorrow morning at dawn. I have to go to the States. I won't be back for a week at the earliest. Let me in, please. I must see you."

"We have nothing to say to each other. Now, go away. You're boring me." She yawned, loudly, near the door.

He rattled the door again, loudly. "Kate, for God's sake—I need you!" His voice seemed muffled by the door, strained and uneven.

"All I need is some sleep," she said lightly. "Don't you know when you're not wanted? Now, good night!"

The silence this time was so long that she pressed her ear to the door, to see if he was still there, and jumped away when she heard his breathing.

"For the last time, Kate," he began thickly, and she cut him short.

"Good grief, you're worse than the Inland Revenue! Haven't you gone yet?"

She heard his heavy footsteps move away, then the slam of his own door.

He had gone, and tomorrow he would not be here when she got up. She would probably never see him again. She sat down on her bed, looking at herself in the mirror. Hollow-eyed, pale, her blonde hair made her look like a negative, strangely ethereal and filled with sadness. How long, she wondered, would this pain last?

CHAPTER NINE

THE rest of the holiday passed, for Kate, in a dull dream. She walked, sunbathed and talked to the others without ever noticing a thing around her. Pallas and Sam were comfortable companions at that time. They asked little of her, seemed hardly to notice the depression which was making her silent and shadow-eyed.

Jean-Paul's grave company was equally peaceful. He would sit for an hour without speaking to her, his smile calm and reassuring when she made the effort to speak. It was with him that she walked over the cliffs, swam and played a slow game of tennis. He was, she sensed, as inwardly troubled as she was, and as grateful for her undemanding company.

Sam did once mention Peter to her, casually, with a brotherly pat on the shoulder. "I can't pretend to be sorry you've given him the air, Sis—Peter's a decent chap, but I never thought he was for you. You want someone with a bit more zing."

She had smiled, briefly, without answering. Peter seemed like someone from the distant past now. She never thought of him, and Sam's comment was an irrelevant intrusion into the turmoil of her emotions.

The two Frenchwomen, Marie-Louise and Hélène, grew bored with Kianthos once Marc had gone, and two days later took off in Marc's plane, which had returned from ferrying him to Athens.

Marie-Louise tried to persuade Jean-Paul to accompany them on her last morning on the island.

Calmly finishing his rolls and cherry jam, her half-brother shook his head. "I am enjoying myself," he said.

His sister threw Kate a hard look. "Why do our men always like to play with pretty blonde dollies?" she asked Hélène, her high voice insolent.

Since she had spoken in rapid French, she probably thought Kate would not understand, but Kate's French although not perfect, was quite good enough for her to comprehend this, and she flushed.

Jean-Paul laid down his knife, wiping his fingers slowly on his napkin. "*Ma chère soeur*," he said coldly, "*tais-toi!*"

The sharpness of the command to shut up made Marie-Louise go rigid with fury, but she said nothing else, and when she came down with Jake, later, her cases packed to go, she said goodbye to Kate with forced politeness.

Jake struggled off, laden with cases. Marie-Louise kissed Mrs. Lillitos, gave Jean-Paul a whispered comment about not forgetting that Kate was ineligible, and departed in a swirl of perfume.

Hélène embraced her mother-in-law more naturally. "I will see you again soon, Maman. I am sorry this has been such a short visit. Next time I will come alone."

Mrs. Lillitos touched her cheek gently. "You must marry again, my dear, and bring your new husband to see me. Paul would want you to be happy. No woman can go through life alone, you know."

Hélène flushed and did not reply.

Kate wished she were going with them. She was aching to leave the island before Marc returned.

"Kate, my dear," his mother said quietly, "will you help me back to my room?"

Reluctantly she obeyed. She had no wish to discuss Marc with his mother, but she sensed that Mrs. Lillitos wished to talk to her about something. But, she thought hopefully, perhaps she is still worrying about Pallas.

Mrs. Lillitos sat down with a sigh of relief. "Ah, that is much better. Kate, sit down near me. I want to talk to you."

Kate drew up a chair and sat down, her hands folded in her lap, her face under control.

Mrs. Lillitos smiled at her, dark eyes soft. "I have grown very fond of you, child. You have a soothing gentle presence—that is why it makes me sad to see you look so pale and unhappy. Won't you tell me what is wrong?"

Kate tried to laugh. "Nothing is wrong, madame. I am enjoying my stay here very much. I like to see Pallas having fun. She . . ."

"Please!" The older woman held up a hand. "Do not try to throw me off the track by talking of my daughter. It is you for whom I am concerned. You look ill. I see that you no longer wear your engagement ring, for instance." The dark eyes rested on her hands, then rose to search her face. "Is this why you are so sad? I had gathered that it was you who broke off the engagement and that you were relieved to do so. Yet you look depressed and lonely. Why is this, Kate?"

"I . . ." Kate broke off, catching her breath, then

went on after a moment, "I expect I have not yet recovered from the attack of sunburn, madame. You have been so kind to me since I arrived. Kianthos is a lovely place. How could I not be happy here?"

Mrs. Lillitos sighed. "How reticent you English are —well, if you will not discuss the matter with me, I cannot be ill-mannered and press you. But remember, Kate, I am ready to talk to you, to listen. And I am very fond of you."

Kate flushed. "Thank you, madame. I . . . I am fond of you, too." She stood up. "You look tired. Shall I call Sophia for you?"

"No, no, I shall sleep later. But run along, by all means, and enjoy your last days here, child. By the way, did Marc tell you—we have decided to take Pallas away from Cheddall?"

Kate was stunned. She halted, freezing on the spot. "No," she stammered. "No, I hadn't heard. You . . . you're not happy with the school? I thought . . ."

"We are very happy with the school, but Marc has decided that Pallas should study music in Paris. He feels she would prefer the Paris Conservatoire to a London school. She is to have special tuition until she is eighteen."

Kate nodded. "I think that is an excellent idea. Pallas will be delighted. Does she know yet? She's said nothing to me."

Mrs. Lillitos shook her head. "No, we have not told her. You can do that if you like. She will take the news better from you. She is very fond of you, too, and I think she will miss you."

"I'll certainly miss her," Kate admitted.

Mrs. Lillitos smiled at her. "But perhaps, who knows, we will be able to see something of you from time to time?" She leaned back, closing her eyes. "*Au revoir, chérie.*"

Kate went downstairs, feeling stunned. If Pallas left Cheddall she would certainly never see Marc again. Had he decided on this change of plan to spite her for refusing to let him come to her room the night he left for Athens?

She found Pallas and Sam playing a strenuous game of tennis, and watched them until Sam won. They wandered towards her, flushed and panting.

"I am exhausted!" Pallas puffed, throwing herself down on the grass.

Sam grinned at her. "Weakling! I could play another game and still win!"

Pallas grimaced at him. "The conceit of him! Did you hear that, Kate? Your brother is absolutely the most conceited boy I ever met!" She aimed a lazy blow at his leg with her racquet, not intending it to land. "Take that, you scoundrel!"

Sam danced out of reach nimbly. "You're just jealous," he observed loftily. "Women aren't called the weaker sex for nothing."

Pallas howled at him, "Male chauvinist pig!"

"Language, language!" Sam teased.

Kate interposed lazily, "Children, children, don't squabble!"

The remark had the desired effect of silencing them both.

She looked from one to the other of them, smiling. Their behaviour strongly confirmed her belief that there was no romantic attachment between them. Only a brother-and-sister relationship could explain the squabbling, the rudeness, the teasing. They were too casual with each other for anything else.

"I just had a chat with your mother, Pallas," she said.

Pallas sat up, tossing back her long black hair. "Oh, yes?"

"She tells me that she has decided to send you to Paris to study music."

"Oh?" Pallas flushed. "When I am eighteen, I suppose, instead of going to a London college of music?"

Kate shook her head. "No, not when you are eighteen. Now. Right away."

Pallas stared at her, eyes wide. "You mean . . . instead of going back to Cheddall?"

Kate nodded. "Yes. Are you pleased?"

Pallas gazed around, mouth open, eyes troubled. "I . . . I do not know. I prefer to concentrate on my music, of course. You know I detest my other lessons. But . . . " she looked at Kate, smiling a little, "I shall miss you, Kate." She grinned at Sam. "And you, you conceited boy!"

Sam said seriously, "I'll miss you too, Pallas. You must write to us from Paris. Lucky you! Imagine . . . Paris in the summer! A lot better than Greyford, I can tell you."

Pallas murmured, "Paris in the summer . . ." Her eyes were dreamy and far away.

Kate wondered if she were thinking about Jean-Paul. He lived in Paris, she remembered. Was that why Marc was sending his sister there? It would be just like him to have thought out such a devious plan.

They went back to the house in a cheerful silence. Watching Sam, Kate was convinced that her news had not upset or worried him. He seemed sorry to be parting with Pallas, but not unhappy.

Jean-Paul was sitting on the verandah. His grave glance rested on Pallas, slight and cool in her white tennis dress, her racquet swinging, her long brown legs moving gracefully.

Kate saw a serious expression move over his face, then he smiled politely, as if at a stranger.

"Good morning again! A good game?"

Pallas linked her arm in Sam's, leaning against his shoulder with an unusually demonstrative gesture. "Wonderful!" she gushed.

Sam gave her a curious look, but said nothing.

When they had gone in Kate looked down at Jean-Paul's bent head. He was frowning slightly, his mouth drawn in at the edges.

"That was for your benefit alone," she said.

He jumped and looked up quickly. "I beg your pardon?" he mumbled, flushing.

Kate smiled at him. "You heard what I said, Jean-Paul," she said dryly.

He shrugged. "I wish I could believe you, but I am afraid I do not agree with your diagnosis. Pallas, it seems to me, is far too interested in Sam. And after all, why not? I like your brother, Kate. A nice boy." He stood up, smiling politely at her. "As pleasant as his sister. I am very glad to have met you, Kate. It has made my stay here a charming one, after all."

"You make it sound so final," Kate said, watching him. "Are you leaving Kianthos soon?"

"Very soon, I think. But I hope I will see you

again, Kate. Will you give me your address? If I am in England I might call and see you, perhaps. Or would you object to that?"

"No, of course not, Jean-Paul. I should like to see you again." She wrote it for him on a piece of paper he found in his pocket. "There you are!"

He put it carefully away. Pallas came out on to the verandah and looked from one to the other of them, her face still very flushed. Kate wondered if she imagined the hurt look in the other girl's dark eyes.

They flew back to England, as scheduled, but Pallas did not go with them. She was to proceed to Paris with Jean-Paul, it seemed. She did not seem to find the news unpleasant, when her mother told her about the plan, although she did give Kate an uncertain look. Kate deliberately avoided any discussion of the subject. Pallas clearly wished to mention it to her but Kate had decided that the less said the better.

If Pallas ever did marry Jean-Paul, she thought, it would be much later than her family had at first intended. That the girl had great fondness for him she no longer doubted. She had watched her carefully and come to the conclusion that Pallas was attracted to him, and valued his friendship. She would probably learn to love him maturely as she grew older. But there was plenty of time for that.

Arranged marriages might have worked well once upon a time, but Pallas had a more modern life in front of her. She would be working like a Trojan for the next five years, at least, and would have no time

for romance. It would be much better to let her discover for herself whether she wanted to marry Jean-
Paul or not.

When they said goodbye, Pallas unexpectedly flung
her arms around Kate. "Goodbye, Kate. Thank you."

Kate hugged her back. "I expect I'll see you again
some day, Pallas. It's been a wonderful holiday. I'm
very grateful to you and your family."

"After what you did for me?" Pallas made a face
at her. "You changed my whole attitude to life. Even
Marc had to agree that that was so! Now look, he is
letting me study in Paris. A year ago he wouldn't
hear of that! It is all your doing!"

"I'm glad I helped," said Kate. Her throat was
dry. So Marc agreed that she had changed Pallas?
She could believe that, but he had not intended to be
flattering, no doubt. He did not approve of the
changes in his little sister.

It was difficult for her to say goodbye to Mrs.
Lillitos. The older woman seemed quietly disapprov-
ing, as though Kate had hurt her in some way. Not
that she said anything to her, but there was a puzzled,
sad expression in the dark eyes as they said their
farewells.

She looked down at the island as they flew far
above it. The sea ran round the shores, deep blue as
the sky, with white frothy foam topping the waves.
The hills and valleys were levelled from up here. It
looked unreal, dreamlike. That was what it was, she
thought. An island of dreams. For her they had been
unhappy dreams, but they had been beautiful, all the
same.

She did not, in the long run, repent or regret anything. She still loved Marc, even though she despised him. He was, after all, a rich and attractive man. No doubt many women, in the past, had been only too happy to amuse him. He could not have realised how differently she felt. She remembered the evening when he had taken her to the Black Swan, the obsequious waiters, the curious stares, the whispering. Living in that artificial atmosphere, it was not strange that for him love should merely mean pleasure, a commodity to be bought like any other.

At least the visit had cleared her mind, shown her the falseness of her relationship with Peter. She might have married him and been disastrously unhappy.

England was oddly noisy when they got to London. Traffic deafened her. People were frighteningly busy and bustling. Cars hooted, pavements were crowded. It was a nightmare.

How quickly one became accustomed to the peace and quiet of an island like Kianthos, she thought. She had lived in an urban atmosphere for most of her life, yet after only two weeks away, she found her eardrums banging with the noise, her head aching, her eyes shrinking from the vivid colours.

It was not that Greeks did not talk loudly. They did. They shouted at each other, in the kitchen at Kianthos. She had often heard the servants arguing, discussing, their gestures and faces lively and dynamic.

But somehow it had all been more good-humoured, less hurried. The pace of life was different.

Her mother embraced her warmly, held her away from her to stare. "My goodness, you do look well!"

Kate laughed, "Do I?" She did not think that that was true. She felt tired and mentally worn.

Then Mrs. Caulfield looked at Sam and exclaimed over him. Brown, healthy, cheerful, Sam looked the very picture of health.

Later, Kate explained to her mother that her engagement was broken. Mrs. Caulfield took it calmly. She did not seem surprised, nor did she ask questions. Kate was relieved, yet wondered why her mother took it so well. Mrs. Caulfield had never, by word or look, hinted that she did not thoroughly approve of Peter. Yet she just smiled and said, "I see, dear," without so much as a blink of the eyes. Kate was puzzled.

On returning to school, Kate had an interview with Miss Carter. The Headmistress seemed quite resigned to the fact that Pallas had left so suddenly after such a short stay at the school.

"I think we did her good, Kate," she said, smiling. "Don't you think so?"

"I hope we did," Kate agreed.

"I'm sure of it—she was very depressed and difficult when she came here, but at the end of term I thought she looked a changed girl, lively, cheerful, full of beans. A great improvement, and I must congratulate you. You did what I expected you to do. Now, did you enjoy your holiday in Greece?"

"Very much," Kate said politely.

After a few remarks about her own holidays in Greece in past years, Miss Carter dismissed her, and Kate went down to her class with a heavy heart. Now, she thought, it's all over. I can forget the entire episode. With Pallas gone, there was nothing to remind her of Marc.

She met Peter in the High Street some weeks later. He was talking abstractedly to a thin, brown-faced girl whose untidy clothes and intense face put her in the student body.

Kate's eyes met Peter's, and he blinked, then smiled, without rancour. "Hi, Kate!" he called, lifting a hand.

She smiled back but did not stop. Some other girl, she thought, was going to have to learn that for Peter the only thing in life was archaeology.

At least the little incident cleared her conscience. It was obvious that Peter was not suffering at all. He seemed perfectly normal.

The next weekend she went to the Lake District, with one of the other teachers, to do some hill walking. The weather was splendid, warm without being humid, and never too hot.

The weekend was very pleasant, and, congratulating themselves, the two decided to do it again sometime. They met a party of fellow enthusiasts on the hills on the Sunday and spent the day with them. All in all, Kate came home feeling very much better.

But her mother looked up as she came into the kitchen, still smiling, and said, "Mr. Lillitos was here yesterday, Kate!"

Kate froze, her eyes for a second out of control, the pain flashing into them before she had time to force a smile.

Mrs. Caulfield straightened. "Kate!" Her eyes filled with concern. "My dear girl, whatever is it?"

She frowned. "Something he did while you were there? Kate, he didn't hurt you in any way, did he?"

Kate laughed, artificially. "Of course not, Mother. What an imagination you've got!"

"Kate, don't pretend with me," her mother said, stricken.

Kate sighed. "I'm sorry, but please, don't let's discuss it. What did M . . . did he want?"

"He wanted to see you," said her mother, watching her uneasily. "He seemed angry when I told him you were away climbing. Wanted to know who you were with—I thought it odd, his asking in such an abrupt fashion. Kate, what's going on?"

"He . . . I . . . Oh, Mother, don't let's discuss it," Kate burst out. "Really, I'd much rather forget him."

She ran out of the room, leaving her mother staring after her with a disturbed expression. She wondered what had happened between her daughter and the tall, dark Greek, to make Kate behave so strangely.

Next morning, as Kate was leaving the house, the telephone rang. Mrs. Caulfield hurriedly shouted after her that she was wanted on the telephone. Kate stood, hesitating. "Who is it?" she asked warily.

"A man with a foreign accent," said Mrs. Caulfield.

Kate looked at the phone with loathing. "Ask who it is, and if it's Marc, tell him I've left for school."

Her mother obeyed, with a worried look, and then said, "It's someone called Jean-Paul, I think."

Kate came back. "Hallo, Jean-Paul!"

"*Bonjour*, Kate," he said quietly. "I am ringing from London, but I am just flying back to Paris. I have little time. I want to ask you if you could come to Paris next week. Pyrakis is giving a concert and I have two tickets. I would be happy if you would come with me."

Kate was astonished. "Well, I . . . Thank you very much, Jean-Paul, but I . . ."

Quickly he interrupted, "I have English friends who would be pleased to put you up for the night. They have a large apartment and only one child, so there is a spare bedroom you could use."

Kate thought hurriedly. "That's very kind of them. Are you sure I would be no trouble?"

"They have said they would be delighted," Jean-Paul assured her. "They are very ordinary people, you understand—a family, but charming and kind. Henry Murray works with me."

Kate said, "I didn't even know you had a job, Jean-Paul!"

He laughed. "You thought I was a parasite? *Mais non*, I am a worker bee, I assure you. I run one of Marc's companies."

"Oh," said Kate flatly.

Jean-Paul was silent for a second, then he said, "But you will come, Kate? I would so like that. And Pyrakis would like to meet you again. I saw him yesterday and he mentioned you with great admiration."

Kate felt herself blushing. "Well, thank you very much, then, Jean-Paul. I would like to come."

"You will fly? Shall I arrange your ticket?"

"No," she said hastily, "I'll do all that. When shall I arrive?"

"Saturday morning, perhaps? I will meet you at Orly if you give me the time of your flight. Drop me a postcard. I must run now. *Au revoir, ma chère*."

"*Au revoir*, Jean-Paul," she said, as the phone clicked.

She turned to face her mother, still flushed. Mrs. Caulfield loked dazed.

"What was all that about?" asked her mother.

"Someone I met in Greece, asking me to Paris for the weekend." Kate kissed her quickly. "Must fly or I'll be late."

"Kate!" her mother called after her, protesting, but she was gone.

Mrs. Caulfield shut the door with a bang. Visits to Greece, trips to Paris for the weekend with strange Frenchmen! What was happening to her daughter?

When Kate got home, she asked her about Jean-Paul, and Kate told her enough to set her mind partially at rest. Kate could see that she was still longing to ask questions about Marc Lillitos, but, since Kate obstinately set her face against discussing the subject, there was little her mother could do but accept the fact.

Kate managed to book a seat to Paris, very early on the Saturday, and wrote to Jean-Paul's Paris address giving the time of arrival.

She was curious about his invitation. Why did he want to see her again? He had no interest in her, she was sure of that. But if so, what was his reason for inviting her?

She left for London on the Friday after school and spent the Friday night in a small hotel near London Airport. Her flight to Paris arrived on time and she came through Customs, carrying her light overnight bag, to find Jean-Paul patiently awaiting her.

He took her bag, smiling. "I am glad to see you again, *chérie*!"

She glanced at him oddly. Suddenly she had a suspicion that he was up to something, but what?

They went directly to the apartment of his friends, to leave her bag there, and Kate liked the friendly English couple on sight. Henry Murray was short, sturdy with brown eyes and a quiet smile. His wife, Clare, had a French elegance coupled with British informality. She chattered easily to Kate, as she showed her to her room.

"It's nice to have someone to talk to now and then. Have you known Jean-Paul long? I like him a lot, but he is a bit deep, isn't he? Doesn't give away much. I wish you could stay longer than one night, but I suppose you've got a job, like the rest of us. Although my job is Sacha. You'll meet him tomorrow morning, I expect. He's a demon—four years old and knows everything! Of course, we christened him Stephen, but everyone calls him Sacha, I don't know why. What lovely hair you've got. Do you mind my saying that? I hope the bed is comfortable. I do hate a lumpy bed, don't you?"

Kate was kept busy just nodding or shaking her head. She did not even try to get a word in edgeways.

After a cup of strong French coffee, Jean-Paul took her out to lunch at an expensive and luxurious restaurant, where she ate a shrimp omelette with green salad, and frothy zabaglione. Afterwards they walked through the shopping streets, Jean-Paul patiently amused as she studied the windows with rapture.

He took her on a lightning tour, in his little red

sports car, round the famous landmarks, then drove her back to the Murray apartment to change.

Clare Murray greeted them cheerfully, carrying a small boy whose freckled face bore traces of jam and butter.

"Hallo, can't stop. Sacha has disgraced himself again—more food on the outside of his face than the inside! Help yourselves to a chair. I'll see you later."

Kate laughed. Jean-Paul stared after Clare with awe.

"She always talks like that," he confided. "And when she speaks French, *ma foi*! It is ten times worse. French is a much faster language than English, of course!"

He left for his own apartment and Kate went to her room to change for dinner before the concert. She had not yet managed to discover why Jean-Paul had invited her. He had not mentioned Pallas, or Marc, or anything but the merest polite small talk. Yet she still felt that he had invited her here for a specific reason.

She wore her white voile dress, as it was now her best dress, and Clare Murray admired it volubly.

Jean-Paul arrived on time, kissed Clare Murray's hand and took Kate off with him to dinner.

"Why did you ask me to come to Paris?" she asked, over their coffee, having decided it was time to be brutally frank.

Jean-Paul's hand hesitated as he lit his cigarette. Then he smiled at her. "I wanted to see you again."

"Will Pallas be there tonight?" she asked flatly.

He flushed. "I . . . I do not know," he murmured without meeting her eyes.

"Jean-Paul!" she reproached him. "It was a good

174

idea for you to make her jealous, but not yet! You really must be more patient. I thought you agreed that you might try again in a few years?"

He smoked nervously, rather red around the ears.

"Well," he began, "you see, Kate, I met her last week, by chance. She was at a party. Pyrakis was talking about you to Marc, and Pallas kept looking at me. She made a joke about you and me! But she was not really laughing, you know? And I thought she seemed . . ." he shrugged deprecatingly, "well, I thought . . ."

"She was jealous!" Kate finished the sentence for him.

"Yes," he admitted. "Kate, I am afraid she will meet someone else at this Conservatoire. She will forget me. I cannot wait!"

Kate said soberly, "But is it right to use me as bait?"

He looked at her apologetically. "You are angry with me? I do not find it easy to talk to most girls, but you are different. I thought you would not resent it."

She sighed. "Well, I don't, as a matter of fact, but I do feel you're trying to rush things. Why don't you just start dating Pallas and go on from there? Take her to concerts, not me."

He stubbed out his cigarette. "I am afraid she will refuse," he said simply.

"You're far too self-deprecating. You're an attractive man."

They discussed it as they drove to the concert, but Kate saw that nothing would make Jean-Paul brave enough to expose himself to Pallas's tongue. His formal education had made him shy and backward with the other sex.

The concert was extremely enjoyable. Kate had never heard Pyrakis play so well. She sat beside Jean-Paul, listening intently and remembering the day she had heard Pyrakis play just for her and Marc. It seemed light years away now.

As they drifted out afterwards she caught a glimpse of a dark head. Her heart thudded harshly and she stumbled slightly, clutching at Jean-Paul's hand.

So it was that when she came face to face with Pallas and Marc, she was hand in hand with Jean-Paul.

Pallas gave them a cold nod. Marc's glittering grey gaze rested on the linked hands, then rose and looked at Kate, contempt and anger in his face.

CHAPTER TEN

PALLAS spoke first, breaking the silence which seemed to lock them all together.

"Hallo, Kate—I didn't expect to see you in Paris!" Then she bit her lower lip, flushing, as if she would like to recall the words.

"The concert was very exciting, wasn't it?" Kate said with artificial enthusiasm. She felt Jean-Paul's fingers growing cold against her own, but he held on tightly, as though afraid to let go.

"Marvellous! How's Sam?" Pallas smiled sweetly. "I do miss him terribly, you know! And he misses me, I know, from his letters."

Kate blinked. She had asked Sam only the other day if he had heard from Pallas and he had said he had not. She knew her brother too well to doubt his word. He would never write to a girl unless she wrote to him first. She smiled, however. "Oh, yes, I expect he does! But he's back at college now, of course." She did not add, as she could have done, that Sam was dating two entirely different beauty queens, one a redhead, the other a statuesque blonde with a Swedish accent and strong Women's Lib views of the world.

It interested her that Pallas was refusing to look at Jean-Paul. He might have been invisible for all the notice she took of him.

Pallas looked sideways at Marc, who was standing

silently listening, his hands jammed in his pockets. "Well," she said, laughing rather falsely, "we must go, Kate. See you some time."

Hating herself, yet unable to help it, Kate let her eyes flicker over Marc's dark, rigid face. Their eyes met. Hers shrank and fell before the look in his. Then he and Pallas had vanished and she was walking out of the theatre with Jean-Paul.

They drove along the riverside slowly, neither in a mood for talking. Kate hardly noticed where they drove after that. By common consent they seemed to drift on in the red sports car, through street after silent street.

When the car stopped Jean-Paul looked up at the narrow house, then at her, with surprise. "Oh, I am so sorry, Kate—I have brought you to my own apartment by mistake." He grimaced. "And it is an error, I assure you, not a trick."

She smiled. "I'm sure it is, Jean-Paul." Then she looked at her watch and gasped in horror. "Good heavens, look at the time! It's two o'clock! What will the Murrays think? I haven't got a key. I'll have to knock them up."

He exclaimed apologetically, "It is my fault! I forgot the time! I am so sorry. But look, come in for a cup of chocolate before you go. I am too tired to think properly but too depressed to think of sleep. The Murrays will understand. After all, one is not in Paris for nothing! They will make assumptions, yes, but charitable ones!"

She hesitated. She did not suspect him of any ulterior motive, but she was wary of all men at the moment. Then she shrugged. Why not? She, too, was too depressed for sleep.

She followed Jean-Paul up into the old-fashioned lift and they whined slowly upwards, coming to a stop with a shudder of machinery. He unlocked a door along the dark corridor and stood back to let her enter.

It was an elegant apartment, very obviously that of a man, yet furnished, she suspected, with the help of Marie-Louise. The curtains and carpets were of a traditional French Empire style. There were delicate pieces of porcelain along the white and gold mantel-shelf. But the furniture was solid and masculine and fitted oddly with the more feminine furnishings.

Jean-Paul gestured her to take a seat, but she said that she would help him make the chocolate. He led her into the tiny kitchen and they companionably heated the milk, talking very little.

"You were right, Kate," he sighed. "She barely looked at me. Well, I am finished after this. I shall ask Marc for a job elsewhere—in England, perhaps."

She stirred the chocolate. "Be more patient," she advised again. "Wait and see. Ring her in a few weeks and ask her out. If she refuses, don't make a thing of it—wait and ask again."

They carried their cups through into the sitting-room and were just sitting down when the door bell rang.

"Who can it be?" Jean-Paul said, staring in surprise. "At two-thirty in the morning?"

He left Kate seated on the sofa, her head back against the fat striped cushions. She ran her fingers wearily through her hair. It was very untidy. Their long drive, in the open-topped sports car, had whipped her blonde hair into a positive birds' nest and she had not yet had time to comb it.

She sipped her chocolate and choked on it as she heard the voice of the new arrival behind her. Spinning round, with a scarlet face and wide, panic-stricken eyes, she faced Marc.

He was grim and furious, his eyes sparking at her. "Quite a surprise," he drawled, jamming his hands into his pockets. "Who would have expected to see you here at this hour?"

"Let me explain, Marc," stammered Jean-Paul, very red.

Marc raised a lazy, sardonic eyebrow. "Do, by all means. I am in the mood for fairy tales."

Jean-Paul looked aghast. "No, no, you misunderstand! It looks odd, I suppose, but truly. . . ."

"Looks odd?" Marc bit off his words with a fierce snap of his white teeth. "You're damned right it looks odd! Let me guess—Kate got locked out and had to beg a night's lodging here? Or she couldn't find a hotel in Paris ready to take her?" He laughed unpleasantly. "Or would it be more accurate to guess that this. . ." he gestured around him, "is the hotel at which she is staying?"

"I am staying at the apartment of Henry Murray," Kate intervened in a clear, cold voice. Her own anger had got the better of her now. How dared Marc burst in here with these wicked insinuations? What right had he? Just because he led an irregular and immoral life it was no reason to imagine everyone else was as bad.

Marc stared at her. "Henry Murray?" he repeated blankly.

"We went for a drive," she explained, "and were just having a drink before we went to bed." Then her last words echoed in her brain and, with a feeling of hot panic, she added hastily, "Before I went back to the Murray apartment, I meant."

Marc's face twitched suddenly, as though he were laughing at her. He looked at her slowly, his gaze mocking. "You need a comb. May I?" And offered her a comb from his inside pocket.

She knew, from the derisive smile, that he would not believe her hair had got rumpled in the drive around Paris. He was quite determined to believe the worst.

Jean-Paul swallowed audibly. "It is unfortunate, the appearance we present, Marc, but you must believe me that Kate and I . . . we were not . . . I mean, there is no . . ." he stammered to a silence, scarlet under Marc's sardonic, cynical gaze.

Kate stood up. "Oh, never mind, Jean-Paul. Let him think what he likes. I'd better go back to the apartment, I think. Will you drive me or shall I call a taxi?"

"At this hour?" drawled Marc. "Allow me—my car is outside."

"No, thank you," she snapped, "I'd rather walk!"

He took her arm in an iron grip. "Now, don't be ridiculous. Why will women take these little things so personally? Good night, Jean-Paul. By the way, are you free tomorrow afternoon? My mother is in Paris for shopping and would like you to take tea with her and Pallas."

Jean-Paul looked at him incredulously, eyes alight. "Take tea? Why, yes, I should be delighted. . . . What hour?"

"Three o'clock? Good. Afterwards you might take Pallas for a drive to Versailles. She needs some fresh air."

Jean-Paul clasped his hands behind his back and swallowed. "I . . . yes . . . I . . ." he stuttered, visibly shaken.

Marc looked down at Kate, his grey eyes mocking her. He marched her to the door and pushed her out in front of him. She maintained a frozen silence while they were in the shuddering, droning lift, but when they were out in the street again, she shook his arm away.

"I'll walk," she announced, turning on her heel.

"Oh, no, you don't," snapped Marc, grabbing at her.

He pushed her into his car and slammed the door. Rigid with fury, she stared straight ahead as he started the car. But within minutes she realised that he was not driving her to the Murray apartment, which was only two streets away from Jean-Paul's, but was heading out of Paris altogether.

"Where do you think you're going?" she asked him angrily.

He did not answer, his face cool and remote in the dim interior of the car, but some minutes later he pulled up at the kerbside, near a small tree-lined square. The wind gently moved the branches of the lime trees, and their cool scent floated in through the open windows of the car.

He turned, one arm along the seat, and looked at

her. Her heart shook. It just wasn't fair that any man should make one feel like this, she thought. With an effort, she made herself sit upright, her chin tilted defiantly.

"Take me back to the Murray apartment," she ordered. She was only wearing a thin shawl over her white voile dress, and it kept slipping down. "I'm cold," she said, her voice reproachful.

He put out his hand and ran it lightly along her thinly covered arm. It burnt through the fine material and she jerked away.

"Don't touch me!"

He stiffened and a glint came into the grey eyes. "I'm tired of this game of yours," he said thickly. "As you seem to expect me to try to seduce you, I might as well be hanged for a sheep as for a lamb, as you say in England!" He leant over her, holding her back against the seat.

Vaguely she thought of struggling, of pushing him away, but the clamour of her senses drowned the voices of common sense. When his mouth lowered to hers, she abandoned herself, heart pounding, and allowed her arms to creep round his neck and touch the dark hair at the back of his head.

He groaned and pulled her closer, kissing her throat and her closed eyes.

"Kate, my dearest," he murmured, "you love me, I can feel it! You couldn't kiss me like this if you didn't love me." His mouth moved back to hers, burning and dry on her lips.

She half sobbed, but responded passionately, unable to resist him. When he drew away again she was weak and drowsy with pleasure. Eyes huge, she stared up at him as he thrust a hand through his hair.

"Why the devil did you hold me off?" he demanded. "Why did you refuse to talk to me the night before I left Kianthos? I was almost out of my mind over you."

"I can't have an affair with you, Marc," she whispered through dry lips. "I love you—I admit it. I wish I didn't. But I'm just not the sort of girl who has casual affairs."

He stared down at her. "Casual affairs? What the hell do you mean? I want to marry you, you feather-brained female!"

She began to tremble violently. "Marry me... you... but... she said...."

"She?" His voice was sharp. "Who said?"

"Marie-Louise," she said miserably. "Oh, Marc, what about her? She said... everyone thought...."

"I wouldn't marry her if she was the last woman in the world," he said forcefully. "She is fun for a party, but hardly the sort of girl one marries. She is all surface, like a painted doll. In the rain the paint comes off. And with Marie-Louise, the glitter comes off when one knows her well enough. So what did she say to you, my silly darling?"

"She implied that you only wanted to seduce me," she said softly, half dazed by her joy, "that you would throw me away when you were tired of me. I couldn't bear it. I was so miserable."

"And that's why you wouldn't let me in that night? You thought I'd come to drag you into bed with me?" He grinned at her. "Was it a struggle, my sweet? Or did you righteously lock your door without a second thought?"

"Don't laugh," she pleaded. "I was desperately unhappy."

He wound his fingers in the silky blonde hair and pulled her close to him, kissing her ear. "I felt pretty fed up myself. I came to ask you to marry me. When you wouldn't even talk to me I felt like smashing the door down. You don't know how close you came to being pretty savagely kissed that night. I lay awake thinking of what I would like to do to you. I couldn't understand your sudden changes of mood."

"I didn't want to love you," she said, sighing.

"That was obvious. I thought, though, that once I had got Peter Hardy out of your life it would be plain sailing. It was a big shock to find I was still not home and dry."

Kate sat up indignantly. "How conceited! You thought that as soon as I was free I'd fall into your arms, I suppose?"

"Something like that," he grinned unrepentantly. "You see, my dear girl, I fell in love with you on our second meeting, when you threw home truths at me like poisoned arrows. Your eyes fascinated me. They were so blue and so cross!"

"You deserved every word!" she said.

"So I did," he agreed lazily, with disgusting complacency. "I knew then that I had to marry you. I had been in love before, but never like that—it was like a thunderbolt. When you told me you were engaged I felt the first qualms. Jealousy was a new experience, and not one I enjoyed. I felt a little better

185

after I had met the gentleman." His derisive tone irritated her.

"Peter is very nice," she said. "I just didn't love him."

"I've no axe to grind about Hardy," he shrugged. "I found him boring, personally," he grinned. "I enjoyed listening to you giving him his marching orders. I knew then that I was right—you didn't love him."

Kate pinched the hand which was fondling her neck. "Vanity, again—you're too sure of yourself!"

Marc looked down at her, his face darkened with a look which turned her bones to water. "I wanted you so much that I just dared not believe you wouldn't feel the same," he said thickly, kissing her throat.

"Oh, Marc," she murmured joyfully, stroking the black hair.

"My mother gave me hope when I came back from the States," he went on. "She was sure you loved me. I came to England after you, but you were away, and your mother seemed so vague about who you were with.... I wasn't certain you weren't seeing Hardy again. I meant to come back again soon. Then I saw you with Jean-Paul."

"Jean-Paul was using me to make Pallas jealous," she explained.

Marc grimaced. "Stupid ass! But why did he break off his engagement if he still loves her?"

She explained and he groaned. "You again! I might have known! But Pallas adores Jean-Paul, you little fool. She has been miserable since we left Kianthos."

186

"I was sure she was reluctant to marry him, though," she explained anxiously.

"I talked to her about that," he said. "She said she was only unhappy because she thought it was a business arrangement—that Jean-Paul did not really love her. He had never breathed a word of any affection to her, of course. It was all done through me. And Pallas hated the idea of an arranged, loveless marriage. But she is attracted to him, all right."

"Oh, dear, I hope I haven't harmed them," said Kate, biting her lip.

"I doubt it," Marc said. "Jean-Paul must convince her he loves her, that's all. She is still very young. He will have plenty of time." He reached for her and kissed her hard. "Never mind them. What about us? When will you marry me?"

"I don't know . . ." She wriggled uneasily. "Marc, we come from such different worlds. Do you think we could make a marriage work?"

He looked very seriously into her eyes. "It has got to work. I need you too much to let you go. Don't start all that again, Kate. I couldn't bear it. When I saw you with Jean-Paul tonight at the concert, holding hands like a pair of lovers, I almost killed him. And I drove back to his apartment, only to find him out. I waited around the corner, where I could see when his lights went on, and then when I got up there, and found you, with your hair all tousled, as though he'd been making love to you . . ." he drew a deep breath, looking savage. "I am amazed at how well I controlled my urge to knock him down."

Kate shivered at the look on his face. "Don't!" she said sharply.

"Then don't you ever again suggest that I could live without you," he said deeply.

She relaxed against him. "Just as you say, my darling," she whispered.

And Marc laughed, softly, and began to kiss her again with a passion that convinced her that any further argument would be a waste of time.

Next day he called for her, at the Murray apartment, and drove her to his Paris home, to meet his mother again. Mrs. Lillitos was overjoyed by their news. She welcomed Kate with open arms, her eyes filled with tears.

"I am so glad! I knew you were the girl for my son when I first met you. The way he looked at you, spoke to you, and of you—I could not be mistaken. But then you told me you were engaged, and I was worried and unhappy. I foresaw grief for Marc."

Marc looked down at Kate with amused eyes. "How right you were, too, Mother! She has given me more headaches than any business deal I ever put through. But I've got her now, and I mean to keep her!"

Kate grimaced up at him. "You talk as though I were a valuable piece of property instead of a person!"

"You are valuable, to me," he teased, and his mocking eyes brought hot colour into her cheeks. "And as for not being a person . . . if you have forgotten how human I can be then I'll have to take you out and show you all over again, and it will be a pleasure, I assure you!"

"Children, children," said his mother gently, smiling at them, "I am too old for such a conversation!

So, Marc, you have invited Jean-Paul to tea? Have you told Pallas that he is coming here?"

Marc shook his head, grinning lazily. "Let it be a surprise for her. I will even ask him to be my best man at the wedding. Will you let Pallas be a bridesmaid, *chérie*?"

"Of course," she said, still very flushed.

Three months later they were married, from her home, and at the reception she watched Pallas, glowing like an apricot in her orange bridesmaid's dress, toasting their health at Jean-Paul's side.

Marc grinned at her, his eyes intimate. "I do not think Jean-Paul will wait too long before following our example!" he whispered.

She nodded, watching smilingly as Jean-Paul put an arm around Pallas and said something to her which brought a flush to her cheeks.

Since their engagement was announced she had seen nothing of Marie-Louise, but she was here today, elegant and provocative in a vivid flame-coloured dress. She had a handsome escort with her and seemed to be enjoying herself. But Kate had no doubts as to Marie-Louise's attitude towards herself. Once or twice the French girl had looked at her viciously, eyes full of hatred.

Nothing could mar her happiness today, though. She slid her hand through Marc's arm and he turned his head to look down at her with that intimate, smiling glance which made her heart turn over.

"Shall we slip away, now, darling?" he whispered. "I'm in a hurry to be alone with you. Three months is a long time to wait for what you want."

Kate flushed and laughed. Moments later she had shed the lacy white bridal gown and was slipping down the back way of the hotel in which the reception was being held.

Marc grasped her hand and they ran to where his car was secretly parked. Behind them they heard cries of whooping pursuit, but they were in the car and away before the guests could catch up with them.

Looking back, she saw Sam waving, and her mother tearfully smiling. Pallas and Jean-Paul stood close together, their hands linked.

"We have both got nice families," said Marc softly, as the car left them all behind.

"Yes," she agreed. "But I know a nicer one!"

He glanced at her, brows lifted.

"The one we're going to start some day," she said, smiling at him.

He drew into the kerb, brakes screeching, and reached for her. "For that remark, my sweet, you must pay the forfeit!" he whispered, as his lips reached hers.

And she gladly paid it.